I0580032

Book Two in the Hacking Wonderland Series
ALLYSON LINDT

Copyright © 2017 by Allyson Lindt
All Rights Reserved
Cover Art by Daqri Bernardo of Covers by Combs

ISBN: 978-1949986419

Manufactured in the United States of America
Acelette Press

Other Books in this Series
Reagan Through the Looking Glass
(Hacking Wonderland Book 1)

For my eternal dragon

Sometimes Sawyer Brolin got tired of the game that went with his persona. Not of games in general, but there were days a guy just wasn't in the mood to be Jabberwock. It was one reason he played the role of one of his own generals for so long—for a change in managerial scenery.

Whispers that someone near the top of his organization was a Fed caused ripples of distrust through his client base. Faking Blake and Reagan's deaths served two purposes—it took them off the radar of anyone else looking for them, and it told anyone who did business with him that fucking with Jabberwock was a suicide pact.

This meeting was another branch of that damage control. Staying a mysterious name with no face was only effective until people asked if the absentee boss truly had control of his organization.

Jabberwock did. So now he had a face, to prove his grip was as tight as ever. That and it took away a hint of Alice's power. She no longer knew a secret about him that no one else did.

He sat across from the owner of the casino

and restaurant they dined in, his smile and gaze never wavering. One of the client's security detail stepped aside at the sound of a phone ringing.

The client hadn't made eye contact in several minutes. "What assurances do we have—?"

"The same you've always had. Have you seen any evidence I can't keep my promises?" Sawyer knew the answer was *no*.

"We'll proceed as planned, then," the casino owner said.

The man who'd taken the phone call returned and whispered in his boss's ear, and the client finally looked at Sawyer. "The young lady you've been looking for is in the casino. She just cashed out her chips and is heading for the elevators. She's registered in one of our high-roller suites, same floor as you, under the name—"

"Thank you." Sawyer pushed back from the table. "We'll continue this conversation later."

He cut a line to the nearest elevators, sidestepping every person who meandered into his path. Her face flashed through his thoughts, cunning but innocent. A living embodiment of contrast. He stepped into an elevator, grateful to share it with only a few people.

Rumors said *she* went by Alice now, rather than Reagan. That was one of the few pieces of information he'd been able to acquire since she threatened to dismantle his organization, six months ago.

The lift doors whispered open, and he strolled down the corridor. He rounded the corner, and there she was, back to him, pulling a key from her purse.

She'd kept the blonde hair, but it no longer hung halfway down her back. The strands brushed her shoulders now.

She was as irresistible as the last time he saw her, but this time she wasn't in another man's arms. Rumors also said she'd left Blake behind. Sawyer was inclined to believe that, since Blake was easier to get a bead on when needed. Sawyer hadn't gone after the former Hatter because he didn't want to send Alice further into hiding.

Sawyer wrapped his arms around her waist. She let out a sigh so soft, it might have been part of the climate control. The scent of violets, familiar all these months later, teased him, and he resisted the desire to bury his head against her neck and inhale.

He couldn't stop himself from gliding his lips along the edge of her ear, though. "The Lion and the Unicorn were fighting for the crown. The Lion chased the Unicorn all around town," he whispered.

"Lion?" She whirled, not breaking from of his grasp. Her body was soft and yielding against his. "Another name?" She raised a brow, and the corner of her mouth quirked up. "How are you keeping track of them all?"

"You tell me, *Alice*."

"I'm glad you were here today." The way she traced her tongue along her bottom lip sent the blood rushing from his head to his cock, and her smile filled his head with the delicious reminder of her moans when she was turned on. The whimpers she made when she came. Her sweet taste when she ground her pussy against his face.

He pressed closer, until his cock dug into her

hip. "You're not very well hidden if you go places you expect to find me. And fleecing a casino owned by a business acquaintance of mine doesn't really live up to that threat you made last time we spoke."

"No. It really doesn't." She shifted against him, making him harder.

This was why she haunted his dreams, despite her threats. He dragged his nose up the side of her neck, falling into her scent. "I missed you." His phone buzzed, and a growl echoed in his skull.

"I can tell. You're vibrating with excitement," she said.

Fucking business. He released her and stepped back to read the incoming message. "It's Queen of Hearts," he spoke as he read. Alice didn't need the details, but he wanted to drive home he hadn't been idle since they last spoke.

"I thought you were the only royalty in your court." Was that surprise in her voice?

Good. He liked keeping her off-balance. "I've tightened ranks, and Dormouse earned a promotion."

"Ah." Alice's shocked tone vanished. "Then we all have new names. What am I calling you?"

"It's not a secret anymore. I'm Jabberwock." The message stole his good mood. *RoseGarden is spewing its secrets onto the internet. "Fuck."* He looked at Alice. Was this her doing? "Apparently, there's a virus on one of our servers. Only one. It's publishing a series of my IP addresses."

Her wide eyes conveyed more mocking than surprise. "Oh my God. How horrible for you."

It was her. He bit back the surge of

amusement, and leaned in. Never touching her, he traced his mouth along her jaw to her lips. "It's nothing that can't be fixed." A millimeter more, and he'd kiss her. Claim that smug, full mouth. Instead, he slipped a tracking device into her purse. "Until next time."

He spun on his toe and headed toward the elevator, not turning to see what Alice did next. He dialed Queen.

"Sir?" Her answer was curt.

Jabberwock stepped into the elevator. Glee danced with irritation. Having Alice back would be fun. Costly, until he won her over, but—fucking hell—the chase would be worth it. "Shut it down. Burn every one of those IP's."

Chapter Two

Blake had always been good at chess. He read the board. Anticipated his opponent's decisions three and five and ten moves out.

Except when it came to Ephraim. Blake sat across from his Marine buddy, the metal of the folding chair hot through his T-shirt. The table between them wobbled each time Ephraim set a piece on the chessboard.

"Have you heard anything about this Reagan woman recently?" Ephraim asked.

Blake studied him, expression blank, but suspicion ticking in his thoughts. "Nothing new. No."

Reagan—he heard she was calling herself Alice now—was probably the one other person who could beat him at this game. She certainly had in the real-life version, keeping him guessing up until the night she left. And nine times out of ten, he'd been wrong.

"Hmm. Let's play," Ephraim said.

Bringing Alice up and then brushing the question aside had to be a tactic to throw Blake off his game. "You're already pulling out the psychological warfare? You must be worried."

For the first couple of months after Alice walked away at that remote gas station, Blake wanted a single answer, nothing more. He wanted to know *why*. Ephraim harped on him, calling him obsessed and addicted. After that, Ephraim had gone out of his way to change the subject whenever her name came up. Until today.

"Doing nothing of the sort. I'll even give you the advantage—I'll go first." Ephraim moved a pawn two squares.

The possibilities for next moves ticked away in Blake's mind, but he was distracted enough to let them run on their own. He made his move and waited.

Blake could count on one hand the people who knew he was alive. He could have gone back to his old life the morning after Alice left. He'd known the moment he returned to the car that she didn't plan to come back. The money on the front seat was his first clue. Someone had seen her walking toward the trucks, but nobody noticed which she got into or which direction she went.

Ephraim moved his pawn diagonally, to capture Blake's, then set the piece aside with a sigh. "First blood."

"Don't sound so thrilled."

Ephraim looked at him. "What would you say if I told you she pinged on my radar today?"

"That's nice." Blake's voice cracked on the casual dismissal. The fury and hurt slamming into him were difficult to hide.

If he'd turned the car around and headed home after he lost her, he could have gone back to the way things should be. Used the fact he knew Jabberwock's identity to earn a promotion and metaphorical gold star. Told his boss Reagan was dead. Gone. Jumped ship. Whatever. The problem was he meant what he told her before she vanished. Not only that he cared—though he hated not being able to get over that—but that he was tired of his old life.

Playing the double agent as a top general for Jabberwock's crime syndicate, showed him that the lines between that and being a government agent were so blurred, they might as well not exist.

"Where'd she show up?" he asked, trying to sound casual. He made his next move, but his mind wasn't on the game.

"Hmm."

A growl slipped out before Blake could stop it. "You brought her up."

"I did." Ephraim danced his fingertips above his pieces but didn't move or focus on any. "I had to see how you'd react. I should have known better."

The cooler in the window kicked on, fan blades groaning in chorus with the adjusting tin trailer. A musty scent brushed over Blake's skin, drying the thin layer of sweat on his skin, but not cooling him.

"I'm not reacting. Whatever you've heard, I'm sure she's moved on by now." Blake forced calm through his veins, searching for that neutral expression that had served him for so long.

He also could have vanished six months ago,

the way Alice did. He was smart when he worked for Jabberwock. He'd stashed money in Swiss accounts—places his employer couldn't find it and Jabberwock couldn't get to it. Blake was set for life, financially.

"How about a wager?" Ephraim moved his next piece.

Blake raised his brows in question.

"You win this game, and I'll tell you everything I heard."

"Deal." The answer burst out faster than Blake wanted.

Ephraim's chuckle was flat. "Your move."

Blake turned his focus inside long enough to lock away all distraction, then looked at the board. Even in November, Arizona wasn't what he'd call a temperate place. A bead of sweat trickled down his back, and another along his cheek. Seconds ticked into minutes and crept on up an hour as he took each move, then waited for Ephraim to counter.

The board held only a few pieces now, and Blake scanned each, potential moves scrolling through his head without effort. *No.* He smiled and slid his bishop to take Ephraim's knight. "Checkmate," he said.

The elation that spread inside should be at beating his friend for the first time. Instead, Alice occupied his mind.

Ephraim scrubbed his face. "I'm not sure I should give you this."

"A bet's a bet."

"You're right." He slid an SD card across the now-barren chess board. "She was in Las Vegas this afternoon. Made sure the cameras saw her and everything. She played a couple of hands of blackjack, then talked to a man with a blond ponytail before she left."

Jabberwock. But that was hours ago, and if she left… The thought went nowhere. Blake couldn't begin to guess what she was up to. The only thing he knew was when she said she intended to tear Jabberwock's organization down from the inside out, the haunting tone in her voice was sincere.

He picked up the memory card and studied it. Did it have the answers he'd wanted for so long? No. Only she did. But it might point him in the right direction. He stood. "I'll be in and out. You'll see. If she's not there, I'm done chasing her ghost. If she is, I'll ask her my question. Either way, by tomorrow night, I'll be on a plane to Fiji."

Ephraim twisted his mouth. "I hope so. For your sake, I pray that's exactly the way things go."

Chapter Three

This was the literal definition of insanity. Blake had looked for Alice in Salt Lake immediately after she left him, to see if she'd reached out to anyone or returned to any of her old haunts. There was no trace of her, because why would she come back here if she was lying low?

Yet here he was again, pulling into the diner across the street where she'd stayed when Jabberwock was *protecting* her—also known as using her as bait to find out Blake was Wonderland's mole.

Blake couldn't find Alice's trail post-Vegas, so he'd come back here, to see if it triggered any other ideas for where to look next.

When he walked through the front door, his feet stalled without permission. She sat in the very back booth, facing the entrance, like she had six months ago. It might be a hallucination, brought on by the same madness that summoned him here. She wasn't the same, though. The set of her jaw was harder, her posture straighter. Her gaze darted from one spot to the next, only lingering long enough to register each, before moving on.

Even in the too-bright fluorescents, mingled with neon reflecting from the signs on the wall, she was as stunning as he remembered. An ache pinged behind his ribs, and he shoved it aside.

When she saw him, she furrowed her brow and drew her lips into a thin line.

Not the reception he wanted, but considering the last time they spoke, she walked out on him, a frown was better than a repeat performance of her leaving. He closed the distance between them and slid into the seat next to her. The cracks in the leather snagged his slacks. Taking this spot was presumptuous, especially when his thigh pressed against hers and the heat from her arm radiated through his shirt.

He did it for the same reason she sat there, though. Clear view of the room, as far from the windows as possible, and shortest, most direct path to the rear exit.

She rested a hand on his thigh and slid higher, tracing her fingers up the inside of his leg.

His cock reacted to her touch, which was familiar and tempting after all this time.

"Is that a forty in your pocket, or are you just happy to see me?" Her voice was low and sultry. She pulled away millimeters before she brushed his erection. "Oh, right. You wear your holster on the other side."

The sarcastic sass was the same as he remembered, but the lack of any other emotion chilled him. "We'll go with *happy to see you*, for now," he said. Was he?

Surprised? Yes. Happy? He should be.

Her chuckle was flat and vanished in the scream of a child a few tables over. "You still know the right things to say to a girl."

"I thought I'd save the alpha-aggressive pickup line a little longer this time." He settled his palm on the table, cringed at the faint tacky sensation, and pulled his hand away again. The place was as charming as ever.

Though the scents of grease and burgers did make his stomach growl, and reminded him breakfast was a pack of mini-donuts from a gas station two-hundred miles south of here.

She took a long swallow of coffee. "You're not supposed to find me yet."

"Do you want me to go out and come back in? Give you fifteen minutes?" Despite the tension running through the conversation, he didn't want to leave. The challenge was as intriguing as the question he wanted her to answer.

"That'd be great…" Her gaze shot toward the entrance, and her back went ramrod straight.

He followed her line of sight. "You need to learn to hide your tension better." His gut soured when he saw what she had, but he kept it from his face. *Dormouse.* And someone he didn't recognize. A guy in his early twenties, who wore a tailored suit, shoes polished to the point they reflected his pinstripes, and a nose piercing.

"I'm not taking advice from you on blending in." Alice slid her fork under the table.

The new arrivals stood near the entrance, staring back, faces hard.

Blake hovered his hand near the holster on his right hip. He didn't want to open fire in here. "I'm guessing you didn't invite Dormouse."

"She's Queen of Hearts, now," Alice said.

He raised his brows, attention never leaving Jabberwock's people. "Alice. Jabberwock. Queen. Everyone has new names now. How clever."

"That's what I said. Does this mean you're going back to being Hatter?" Alice's laugh was more genuine this time. Disconcerting, given the circumstances.

The hostess showed Dor—Queen and her companion to a booth. Queen's stare never wavered.

"We need to get out." Blake was familiar with the layout of the place, and he'd made Alice memorize it last time they were here. The back hallway led toward the restrooms, then cut through the back corner of the kitchen.

Alice's leg tensed against his. "My car is by the rear exit." What was she up to?

"She won't open fire. Not in here." *Never draw unwanted attention.* That was one of the key things drilled into Blake's head while he worked for Jabberwock.

"Things have changed," Alice said.

"Not this."

Queen's companion drew a pistol, as if taunting Blake. Blake grabbed Alice's arm and yanked her down a second before a gunshot ricocheted through the diner and plaster exploded over their heads.

He shoved her toward the exit. "*Go.* Right behind you."

Screams overlapped his words. The chaotic mix of people running, ducking, and staring provided the mess Blake and Alice needed, to duck outside.

It was a quick sprint to the exit, but Alice pulled up short the moment she burst through the back door, and Blake had to stumble or risk colliding with her.

Queen was waiting.

"See?" Alice asked. "Gunfire."

This hardly seemed like the time. "I stand corrected."

Queen rolled her eyes, making him think she felt the same. She looked at Blake. "Sorry about Knave. He's got an itchy finger."

Great. *Now* they were being polite.

Alice launched herself into a spinning kick and landed more than a foot from the other woman.

"What the fuck was that?" Queen asked.

Blake tensed, looking for the perfect opening. That flash of distraction. If it appeared, it wouldn't be for long.

Alice shrugged. "That was disappointing. I'm demanding my money back—"

Blake sidestepped the Queen and landed his elbow in her windpipe.

"—for those Kung Fu lessons." Alice sprinted away from the gasping woman and toward a Ford Taurus.

She had the engine running and car in gear when Blake slid into the passenger seat.

He risked another look at her, surrealness mingling with the adrenaline rushing through him. She'd changed so much, but she was still Alice. It was stunning and terrifying.

She navigated toward the neighborhood streets instead of the main roads, taking twists and turns without hesitation. She reached an intersection that indicated one direction was the interstate and the other led to a dead end.

Blake's stomach dropped into his shoes when she turned toward the *No Outlet* sign. "Alice?"

She downshifted, keeping the car at a high RPM. "I've spent a lot of our time apart not being spotted. You've spent the same window flitting between here, Arizona, and Nashville, with occasional trips to Rome. I know my way out of this neighborhood."

He had no idea how his activities were related to her knowledge of the roads, but he bit his tongue about any more navigation choices.

A moment later, she turned into a parking lot, hopped a low curb at the other side, and merged into traffic heading onto the freeway.

"You weren't supposed to find me yet." She reached cruising speed in a matter of seconds and wove through traffic swiftly and smoothly.

"So you mentioned." They were going to have this conversation now? While there might or might not be someone pursing them? "You weren't supposed to leave me."

"You spent two weeks lying to me." She spoke through clenched teeth. Every few seconds, her gaze twisted to each mirror in turn before falling back on the road.

"Because I didn't have a chance to explain." It sounded like a weak excuse now. He could have found time to say *something.* "You kept your secrets."

"To save my life. And it was *a* secret. Singular."

"Technically, the most important fucking thing you could have known." He bit the inside of his cheek, to keep his anger from rising. He wasn't mad at her; her reasons were solid. He was furious at himself, for missing so many truths back then.

She cut across three lanes of traffic, amid the blare of horns, took the next exit, and pulled into a gas station. "I disagree. He was a threat regardless of his identity, and your knowing didn't change your actions." She shut off the engine and stepped from the car.

He did the same, looking around to determine *what next.*

"Catch." She tossed him a set of car keys the moment he spun. "It's the white Corolla. You drive." She walked away from the Taurus, leaving the keys on the front seat.

Any other day, under any other circumstances, he'd get her door. Right now, it seemed low priority. "You know I'm not some super-highly-trained car-chase expert, like in the movies."

"I figured. But you typically have good situational awareness, and I need to figure out where I'm going next, since my current plan is fucked up. And I need to send a text."

"To whom?"

She looked at him over the roof of the car. "You and I don't have the kind of relationship where I give you that information. How about this? It's not someone who's a threat to you."

That would have to do for now. How had she changed so much, in such a short amount of time? And was there enough of the free-spirited Reagan in her that she'd come out of this situation and still remember who she used to be?

Chapter Four

Police seek man for questioning in diner shoot-out.

The headline scrolled across the bottom of the cable news-channel's feed.

The wheeled office chair Sawyer sat in creaked when he leaned back. Scrubbing his face, he exhaled nosily through his fingers. When he straightened again, the breaking news hadn't changed. A variety of camera angles flashed on screen, each featuring the diner where Queen and Knave were supposed to find Alice.

Several grainier shots of Knave mixed with the high-quality footage. Cell-phone videos of the man who opened fire in a crowded Salt Lake City restaurant.

The scents of jet fuel and asphalt mingled with Sawyer's growing fury. He needed to be back home, rather than at the windowed office of a private runway, so he could lock himself in the basement and go a few rounds with the seventy-five pound body bag.

His phone buzzed. An encoded message from

Queen.

We're here.

Good. He stood, smoothed out his suit, and picked a ball of white fuzz from his jacket sleeve. When he was certain the ice on the surface hid the fire raging underneath, he stepped into the hanger.

November air gusted through the vast space, but it didn't cool him. A moment later, Queen and Knave walked through a door a few feet away.

Queen—Lisa—held herself straight and tall, expression impassive. Exactly what Sawyer expected from his oldest friend. She might let the mask slip sometimes, in private, but she had the most impressive poker face he'd ever seen.

Knave wouldn't look him in the eye. His hand kept twitching toward the inside of his jacket, which Sawyer noticed was lacking a holster or gun. Lisa had already disarmed him and—knowing her—disposed of the weapon.

When they were a few feet away, Sawyer spoke. "You were there to do observation." He kept his tone low and even, and his gaze on Knave. "Ob-ser-vay-shun. Do you need me to define that?"

"No, sir." Queen stood with her back ramrod straight, feet shoulder width apart, and hands clasped behind her, like a soldier at ease, waiting for her next command. The deference was for show; she always adopted it in public. Another reason he trusted her to keep his secrets.

"Then *why* is Knave the hottest thing on cable news?" It was a rhetorical question. Knave was incapable of holding out when it was required. Why the fuck didn't Sawyer send someone else to keep an eye on Alice? "She bolted. Didn't she? Took one look at you and ran?"

"Correct." Queen bit off the word.

The low burn inside Sawyer grew, the longer he thought about the monumental fuck-up of the situation. "We finally had her, and she fled."

Knave stepped toward him but stopped short when Sawyer raised his brows. "She wasn't alone." A thread of indignation ran through Knave's retort. "I thought we'd kill two birds—"

"You're not supposed to kill *any* birds." Sawyer's voice echoed off the metal siding of the vast room. "Who was she with?"

"That's why I shot. She was with Hatter, and I know you want him out of the picture."

Sawyer let out a long hiss, counting to ten and forcing the calm through his veins. "I want him *in* the picture—as in shackled and standing about where you are." His phone buzzed. "Excuse me." He swiped *Answer* and turned away to speak into the phone. "Yes?" He wasn't worried about having his back to the trigger-happy Knave. Not with Lisa behind him.

"After today's news, we've decided to go with another negotiator," a voice, masked by a synthesizer, said.

If the inferno inside grew any hotter, Sawyer was going to burst. "I understand. You do what you must. Cheshire Cat?"

"Not that it matters, but yes. We won't be in touch again." The line went dead.

"*Fuuuuuck.*" Sawyer flung his phone at the concrete, and it shattered at his feet and scattered in a dozen pieces. He'd been in the middle of a different conversation. He turned back to Knave. "The man's name is Blake. You betray the post, I retire the fucking title. You, for instance."

Knave sneered. "I didn't betray you; I'm not stupid."

Sawyer glanced at Queen, who gave a nod so slight, she might have been her shifting her weight. He turned away as the ear-splitting *crack* of a gunshot filled the air.

And that was the real reason he called her Queen of Hearts now. The woman was an effective fucking executioner. "You coming?" he called as he strode toward the jet waiting on the runway.

"Of course." She fell into step next to him, phone in hand. She raised the device to her ear and spoke. "We need a clean-up crew. Standard hanger. Airport Two… That's correct… Thank you."

Efficient all around.

Without the walls to block the gusts of incoming storm, the cold bit through his jacket and slacks. He let the weather drag away the cloud of irrationality that threatened him, as he climbed the steps to the plane.

The scent of sanitized-everything helped draw more of the flames from his mind. As he settled into his seat, soft leather molding to his body, he grasped calm and focused on it.

Lisa took the spot across from him, and they prepared for takeoff. She didn't say anything, and he was grateful for the silence as the plane taxied. He fell into the vibrations of wheels on the runway, then the drop of his stomach as they left the ground.

He looked at her. "Do we have a bead on

Alice again?"

"No. The tracking signal is still coming from the diner."

"She wanted us to find her." He spoke to himself as much as to Lisa.

She scowled. "You don't know that."

It made sense, though. "She didn't discover the tracking device *after* the shooting started. Did she leave her purse behind?"

"No."

"It wasn't a coincidence she was in that place, with Blake. She knew she was being tracked before she arrived."

Lisa stood and took a few short steps to reach the mini fridge and bar, hidden behind wood paneling at the back of the passenger cabin. "Maybe. Drink?"

She'd never made it a secret that she thought he gave Alice too much credit, but Alice had successfully hidden from Sawyer until she wanted to be seen. Maybe she wasn't that clever, but he had to be cautious.

"I'm good," he said.

Lisa dropped into her seat again, holding a glass with ice and what he assumed was Diet Dr. Pepper. The only time she dropped the ice-queen mask was when she and Sawyer were alone. Then again, he'd reached that same point. "What now?" she asked.

"Business as usual, including continuing to look for Alice."

She raised her brows. "Because that's worked so well for us so far." Sarcasm sliced her words.

Sawyer was unconcerned. "Five hundred

bucks says she'll seek me out again soon."

"I'm not taking that bet."

He smirked. "Because you know I'm right."

Chapter Five

Alice fitted a key into a tarnished doorknob, wiggled it a few times, and turned. She pushed open the motel room door. "Welcome to my temporary home."

"Here?" Blake stepped inside, and she followed, locked, and latched up behind them. If he reached out from here, he'd touch the bed. A few steps past that, and he'd run into the far wall.

She tossed her wristlet on the bed. "Don't knock the accommodations. They take cash, and their guest registrations are paper, not digital."

"It's not that. God knows I'm not picky. But I didn't think you'd ever lock yourself in a cramped room again."

She sat on the edge of the bed and the browns of the comforter crinkled around her, merging into a nauseating array of blandness. "The important part of that statement being *yourself*. I'm here because I chose to be; I hold the key. Besides…" She shook her head.

"What?"

"Never mind."

The heat kicked on, blowing a gust of what smelled like burning dust through the room. He studied her as she examined her feet. "Alice."

"Please don't." She looked up, meeting his gaze. "Yes, it's the name I give most people now, but I can't. Not from you. I need— Call me *Reagan*, please." Despite the firm tone, a tremor of hurt ran through her voice. Her expression slipped for a blink, the lines around her mouth softening, before her mask slid back into place.

What did she mean, *not from you*? "All right. Reagan it is." Was there a way to get rid of that ache, but still bring back the rest of the old her?

She sighed. "I was going to say, as far as the room, the two-hundred dollars I took from you didn't go far, and I've learned there are a lot worse places to sleep than a small motel suite or even an interrogation cell."

"I'm sorry."

"Don't be." She summoned a smile bright enough, it almost chased away the tinge of gray that clung to everything in the room. "You tried to help me. You lied in the process, but you tried." A shudder raked over her. "Anyway. It's in the past. How did you know where I was going to be today?"

He pulled out the chair next to the desk, spun it, and managed to maneuver it to where he could sit without brushing his knees against hers. "I'd like to say something clever about following the clues or Jabberwock's people. Really, I got lucky. A friend picked up your image in Las Vegas, and I hoped you'd touch base at home if you came out of hiding. I was only at the diner because that's the street I turned down when I got into town. I guess my subconscious wanted to go back to where we got to know each other."

"Except for that bit where you lied about who you were."

"And you know why I did that." It was going to be a long time before he lived down the secrets he'd kept from her.

"I do know why. Do you understand why I left like I did?"

No. But he did know. He'd waited all this time to see her, telling himself the only reason was because he wanted to ask her *why*? But he had that answer already.

After what she'd gone through—her professor's death at the hands of the people he worked for, the lies that kept her tossed back and forth like a chess piece rather than a person, the various flavors of psychological torment she was subjected to… And he was associated with all of it. Worse— when he had a chance to come clean, he didn't.

"Yeah. I do understand. I missed you." The second thought wasn't related at all to the first, except that he'd never admitted either to himself before.

She caught her bottom lip between her teeth, and her scowl melted into mischievousness. "You missed the sex." She straddled his legs and draped her arms over his shoulders.

"Reagan." The rest of his protest blurred into the back of his mind when she shifted in his lap.

"Be honest. And don't go off on any sort of *this isn't the way to distract yourself* or *you don't know what you're doing.*"

Fucking hell. "I'd never question for a moment whether you knew what you were doing. And yes, it was good sex. Or incredible."

"Agreed." Her voice was a purr. "I've heard sex is a good way to burn off excess adrenaline." Each time she adjusted her weight, she pressed against his cock at a new angle.

He was rock hard, digging into her. "It *has* been an intense day. I could use a way to wind down, if that's what you need."

"*Need* is the perfect word for it."

He could protest more. Tell her he was only here for one answer, and he had it now. He didn't have any illusions this meant something to her.

He could put up some sort of front, about this being a bad idea. Say he didn't want to take advantage of her. But they'd covered that, and he wasn't a good enough guy to talk himself out of sex, when there was a willing offer on the table. He knotted his fingers in her hair, eliciting a gasp. The sound slid over his skin like silk, and he nipped her bottom lip before claiming her mouth.

She dragged her nails down his back, raising goosebumps on her way. She tasted like coffee and obsession when he twisted his tongue around hers in a dance. He stashed the outside world, to dive into the now.

Blake shoved up Reagan's shirt, and she broke away to let him tug it over her head and toss it aside. He looked her over, trailing his gaze along the curve of her waist and the swell of her breasts under her bra.

"What?" Her flush traveled down the pale

skin of her neck.

"Appreciating the view." He nipped her shoulder, then drifted lower, licking a path down her chest.

He unhooked her bra, needing to get closer. When he dragged a thumb over her nipple, she arched her back, grinding against his erection. He lowered his head and took the pink nub in his mouth, to suck and nibble.

"Fuck." She gripped his hair, holding his head captive.

He increased his attention in time with her moans. Each time he licked, she squirmed harder in his lap.

"You're going to make me raw," he said with a strained chuckle. "I can't do this teasing thing." Hands on her hips, he lifted her.

She squealed and giggled. That was an incredible sound, and it chased the real world further into the background. He used his body to nudge her toward the bed, stripping off his shirt as they moved. The heat of her bare chest against his sent flames racing through him.

She hit the mattress and fell backward. It was the perfect opportunity to pull off her jeans, before setting his hands on either side of her head and ducking in for another long kiss.

How could he have missed this so much, having only had one night with her? Whatever the cause, this taste ignited his desire. He had enough grip on his reason to grab a condom from his wallet, before losing his pants.

He rolled on the protection. This was

probably a bad idea.

He shoved the reservation aside. "I want you on top of me."

"I like that." She straddled him when he lay back.

He fisted his dick and dragged it along her slit. The easy slip pinged in his nerve endings. He couldn't wait any longer. He thrust his hips up and slid inside her.

"Fuck, you feel good." His voice sounded ragged to his ears. It wasn't just the tight, wet grip on his shaft; it was *her*. The energy pulsing between them squeezed around him.

The way her eyelids fluttered each time he pounded inside her drove straight to his gut and tightened in his balls. He bit the inside of his cheek, hoping the sting would help him hold out longer.

He sought out her clit, and when he traced circles over it with his thumb, she gasped and pressed harder against him. Her weight, her gyrating... it pushed him to the edge. Every inch of him pleaded for release.

Not yet.

He increased his pace both with his thrusts and his attention to her sex.

She gripped his hand, digging in her nails, and tilted her head back, eyes closed tight. When she came, her pussy milked him.

The blend of her cries of pleasure, her slightly parted lips, and every sensation raced over him. He couldn't hold back any longer. He came hard, grunting and hammering against her.

He kept thrusting as long as he could, wanting

to fall into this feeling a little more. When he finally slowed to a stop, she leaned forward and rested her head on his chest. Neither spoke for several minutes, and he was happy to sink into the closeness.

As the outside world rushed back in, his thoughts flipped in on themselves. He'd lied to himself for the last six months about being able to walk away from her. It would have taken years to forget Reagan, and now that he had her back, he'd do anything in his power to keep her, and to keep her safe.

She rolled off him and curled up against his side. Her hot breath fell across his chest, and her eyelashes teased his skin. "You should know"—her voice was so quiet, he has to strain to make out the words—"I'm going back to Jabberwock."

Every muscle in body tensed until the tendons in his neck threatened to snap. "*What?*"

Chapter Six

Blake struggled to process Reagan's revelation. To stay objective and removed. Sex didn't make her his. That wasn't his issue with the news, though. He bit back the, *Are you fucking insane?* that tried to propel itself out. "He's not going to trust you."

"I don't expect him to." She rolled away and stood. The dim light in the room cast her curves in silhouette. He wasn't going to stare. He didn't need the distraction. "He's not going to push me away, either."

"How do you know that?"

She strolled the few steps to the bathroom. "Because he prides himself on outthinking those around him." Her response mingled with the sound of running water. "The longer he tries to guess what I'm up to, the more effective this becomes."

Blake stripped off his condom, wrapped it up, and tossed it in the trash. "And what is *this*? What kind of top secret plan do you have?" He moved to the bathroom to clean up, and she brushed past him, on her way out.

This was too clinical, and she was too detached. *Casual sex. Remember?* He had to keep that in mind.

"The point is to make him question everything and everyone," she said when he rejoined her. She had dressed. "To get him to destroy himself." She walked to the dresser, snagged a small holster from the duffel bag on the ground, and clipped it to her hip.

A taser. Blake should probably be grateful she wasn't drawing it, given the edge to her words. He yanked his clothes back on and sat on the edge of the bed. "That's almost as bad as the plan to promise not to tell anyone who he was if he let you go."

"That was a good idea that needed refining. He let us walk, didn't he?" She shoved a few things into a duffel bag. Not that there was much in the room that wasn't bolted down. "This is what he does. He reads people, he makes decisions based on it, and he spends his time trying to stay one step ahead of everyone."

Reagan shouldered her bag and turned to face him. "What was it the two of you told me? He rearranged his entire organization to find out who you were working for and prompt you to make a mistake. The entire fucking organization."

He didn't have an argument against that. After the atrocities he'd seen Jabberwock execute—torture, mutilation, dismemberment—without flinching, that was a mind Blake didn't want to delve too far into. It concerned him that Reagan seemed to do so with ease.

"Why?" Blake asked. "What's driving your

obsession?"

"He used me. I'm a random person, and he didn't hesitate to shove me into the middle of the chaos. He subjected me to psychological manipulation. Lies. To get at someone else. And I realize the Feds did the same, and worse—I won't ever forget that week—but Jabberwock does it so he can rule an empire of lies and deception. He did all that for power. For wealth. Mostly power. So he could sit on his throne, untouched and holy."

Her cheeks were flushed red when she finished, her brow was furrowed, and her jaw clenched.

"The notion still feels incomplete." Blake couldn't ignore the venom in her voice. Talking her out of this didn't seem like an option. "What aren't you telling me?"

"A lot of things. I've been watching. I found some information from Alex."

Her brother. Blake grasped more pieces of an incomplete picture. "What kind of information?"

"The kind that propels me forward."

So much for getting that answer out of her. "At least you're not relying solely on a headfuck, to do whatever it is you're up to."

"As far as he's concerned, I am." Reagan chewed the inside of her cheek as she searched Blake's eyes. "Alex hid some things—details—but scattered. Not all in one place. He implied it's enough to take down Jabberwock."

"Take him down, how?" Blake wanted more details on where she was getting her information, but he was aiming for questions he hoped she'd answer.

She growled. "If I knew that, I wouldn't be here still. I need more information, in order get to the final conclusion. For instance, Jabberwock told me—" She snapped her jaw shut. "Why am I telling you any of this?"

Blake wondered the same thing. "Because it sucks to go it alone. Because you've chased it in your head so long, you need a sounding board? Because saying the words aloud forces you to assemble them differently?" All things he'd struggled with when he was inside Jabberwock's organization and trying to make sense of Wonderland.

"Most of it isn't news to you, anyway. Jabberwock told me Alex was stashing money for me, for college. That he did so much of what he did for me."

"But you attended on a full scholarship. Hell, half the time, your bank account was overdrawn."

Her scowl deepened. "It's going to be a long time before I'm okay with how much you know about my past that I didn't tell you. But it helps make my point. If you know that, he knows it. I rarely saw money from Alex. He sent me fifty bucks here and there, and he was gone before I made it through my freshman year. He didn't leave me anything, that I saw."

"Why would Jabberwock tell you that, if he didn't believe it? If he realized you'd know better?" Blake had an idea of what the answer was—the guy specialized in games. This was more, though. What was Blake missing?

Reagan fidgeted with the handle of her duffel bag. The heat sputtered a few times, before kicking on and spewing burnt dust and filter into the room again. Voices carried through the door, drawing closer, then farther away.

She glanced over her shoulder at the noise, then looked back at Blake. "Because he thinks I'm hiding the money. That's the only thing I can figure that makes sense. A guy who tells as many half-truths as Jabberwock does, believes everyone else does the same. Alex implied there are accounts, so my guess is either Jabberwock hasn't found them but knows they exist, or he has found them, and someone who's not me or him is making withdrawals."

It was convoluted, but so were a lot of things about the way Wonderland operated. This was simple, compared to some of the surreal things Blake saw during his time as Hatter.

"Anyway. I'm on my way out. You can stay in the room if you want. Do whatever," Reagan said.

"We're still talking." He grabbed her wrist, and she hissed.

She whirled and wrenched free from his grasp, focusing an angry glare on him. "We're done, because you don't trust me, and that goes both ways. I'm doing this alone."

"No, you're not." He had the answer to his original question, *Why did you walk away?* It was time for him to go, but he couldn't let her head into whatever this was by herself. His sticking around was to keep her safe, and hopefully to bring her back from the dark edge she teetered on. Nothing more.

"I'm not asking for your input. Are you going to handcuff me, to keep me here? Because… kinky." Her wink looked out of place in the middle of her scowl.

Under other circumstances, it would be tempting. "You're right. I can't stop you from leaving, just like you can't stop me from following. If you don't want another coincidence like in the diner, it would help if we were on the same page."

Hesitation whispered across her face before vanishing behind a stone mask. "Fine. Follow." She grabbed the car keys. "I'm taking I-80 to Iowa or so, then cutting south to Nashville. Hope you can get a ride fast." She reached for the door.

"You're driving to Tennessee?"

She paused. "I don't have ID. Staying off the radar, and all that. I drive everywhere and make sure I don't get pulled over."

"I can get us on a flight, and no one will question it."

"Not that I'm interested, but how?" She let her duffel bag slide to the floor.

"I know someone who can have us law enforcement badges in a matter of hours."

"How is that supposed to be better?" she asked.

"Law enforcement who need to fly with a firearm don't go through security. If we're flying out during peak hours, no one is going to look too closely at us. We'll be processed and waved along. Nothing recorded. No one giving us a second glance."

"Your connections haven't kept you off the radar." Despite her arguments, she stepped away from the door.

"Does it matter? You want Jabberwock to know you're coming, right? You don't want to be stopped by someone else first?"

"I'd rather he not be expecting me." She grabbed her bag again.

"In three days? Two, if you drive straight through without sleep?" Blake stood and joined her. "How useful will you be if you show up exhausted and jibbering?"

"My plans are flexible. I can adjust if he diverts."

"All right. Go." He was out of ways to persuade her, short of *actually* using handcuffs. Perhaps he should have brought a pair.

Reagan chewed on her bottom lip. "We go through security while the airport is packed, and no one knows our real names?"

"That's the plan."

Her shoulders slumped. "All right. I wouldn't mind backup from you, I guess. And free peanuts would be nice." She settled into the chair.

He wanted to fist pump but settled for a tight smile. "I'll make some calls."

Chapter Seven

Sawyer hated to lose the condo in Seattle, but when Reagan vanished overnight, he needed to implement security precautions. He hadn't known whom she'd told or what had happened to her.

He and Lisa arrived at his actual home base—a house outside of Atlanta. One of the few places he could be himself, and a spot no one associated with him except for her.

"I'm going to ditch my bags and change," Lisa said as they entered the kitchen through the garage.

"Sounds good. Meet you in the war room in fifteen?"

She gave a short nod and headed down the hall toward her room. Neither of them spent enough time here to consider it *home*, but it was as close as they got.

He climbed the stairs to the second floor—his sanctuary. Ten minutes later, he'd exchanged the suit for a T-shirt and sweat shorts, and was walking into the room at the back of the house.

If he decided later he still wanted to go a

couple of rounds with the punching bag, he was dressed for it. Lisa had her seat staked out on a beanbag on the other side of the room. She'd shed her work uniform for a tank top and yoga pants.

Sawyer bypassed the desks against the wall and a couple more beanbags, and grabbed himself a spot on one of the couches. He plugged a network cable into a port hidden under a spot in the floor, and the other end went into his laptop.

There was no wireless in here. It wouldn't travel through the copper-lined walls even if it were an acceptable risk. "Do we have an assessment on the residual damage from Alice's network prank?" he asked.

Lisa didn't look up from her computer. "She used a back door."

Which was the top possibility, but it didn't explain— "How did she get it on the server?"

"Do you want solid facts or my best guess?"

He didn't like the sarcasm. It meant she didn't have *solid facts*. How did Alice do this without leaving a trace? "Best guess."

"She piggybacked it on an update for something widely used, embedding it well enough that everyone has it but she's only using it on us."

"She's not that good." Was she? No. She might have considerable skill, but not better than what he and Lisa did when they put their heads together.

The beanbag creaked beneath Lisa as she leaned forward. She set her laptop aside and rested her forearms on her knees. "You don't know that. Besides, she doesn't have to. Guess what else I found?"

"Not in the mood."

"You can be Oscar the Grouch now, too. Fantastic." Lisa rolled her eyes. "After Vegas, I sent out a crawler, to check the high-roller suites for all of our contracts. It's hard to tell for sure, but based on patterns and the security footage they keep in the cloud, she's playing a different casino's tables every other weekend. She's dropping tens of thousands and winning ninety percent of the time. This has been going on for at least a couple of months, and I assume as long as six months total, not counting the big-spender tables."

He tilted his head back and stared at the ceiling, letting out a long groan. "So she can count cards. Your point is?"

"She's not hurting for cash. Whatever she can't do, she can pay someone else for."

Not as interesting as if Alice did the work herself, but it was something he didn't expect from her. "Send me what you have and check the traps."

"Will do."

Seconds later, he had the information Lisa had gathered, and her fingers flew across her keyboard. The *traps* were a series of crawlers always scanning for anyone looking for Jabberwock. The methods had been refined over time, to make the process more accurate, but details needed to be manually vetted, and pursued or discarded.

When Sawyer and Lisa started this, she let him take the lead. As she put it, *I'm not a deal maker.* Sawyer had been burned twice now, by Alex and then Blake. Lisa was the only person he trusted.

"Remember we have a business to run." Her comment jarred him out of his thoughts, and the edge in her voice caught him off-guard.

He studied her for a moment and raised a brow. "What does that mean?"

"If you spend your life pursuing Alice, you're the one who's going to fall down the rabbit hole."

Irritation snaked through him. "She hacked my fucking network. I'd like to know how, and stop her from doing it again."

"*Our* network." Lisa glared at him. "I'm not saying you're wrong, Mr. Defensive; it's a warning. Watch yourself."

"I get it." He spoke through clenched teeth. The exchange climbed under his skin and settled in, along with the heavy mood in the room.

He tried to focus on the new information about Alice's activities, but Lisa's comments nagged his thoughts. When his phone chimed, he grabbed it, grateful for the distraction.

Hearing whispers about Cheshire Cat.

When he read the message from Three, he realized he shouldn't have been so eager. The Heart was in Tokyo, investigating a potential client.

Keep an ear out. Let me know, Sawyer replied as Jabberwock.

When Jabberwock agreed to work with someone, he'd already done his research. He reviewed every corner of a person's life online. He had a knack for finding the subtleties in people and their digital interactions.

It was the reason he'd trusted Blake when he let him into the organization, besides the bland past, which was apparently doctored. It took Blake years to work his way up the ladder, but when it was time for Sawyer to replace Alex, Blake had proven himself.

Sawyer had still worked with Blake—Two of Clubs at the time, a simple grunt—over the course of several jobs before he named the trio *Hatter, Hare,* and *Dormouse.*

It was also why he let Blake leave with Alice. It didn't matter whom Blake worked for; he didn't see the world in the black and white that would drive him back to the side of law enforcement.

Speaking of Blake—Sawyer knew where he'd been for the last six months, and it wasn't with Alice. So why was he at the diner?

Another message chimed through from Three. *They're talking about some shooting in the US. They've said Jabberwock several times.*

So Knave's itchy finger had gone international. "We need to do damage control PR on this shooting in Salt Lake," he said.

"You're on that, then?" Lisa sounded annoyed. "Checking the traps."

His email pinged. It was a dummy account he'd set up for client interactions, and the message was from the same group Three was watching in Japan. *Cancelling the contract.*

"*Mother fucker.*" Sawyer slammed his fist into the cushion next to him.

Lisa jumped. "What now?"

He reeled his reaction back in. "This isn't right." How did they know Knave was his? Pieces ticked against each other in his head, looking for a way to click. There it was. What were the odds that two different clients, in two different parts of the world, canceled on the same day?

Knave's mistake made the news, but the second instance *just happened* to be while Three was watching, and they *just happened* to be discussing that very thing within ear shot, and *just happened* to cut the contract moments later. "We lost Tokyo."

"What?" Lisa's voice rose in volume and pitch. "Why?"

"Do you want solid facts or my best guess?"

She pursed her lips. "Clever. What's your guess?"

"Cheshire Cat. We need to know who the fuck it is."

"Alice."

He gave a dark laugh. "You think you're funny, but you're not. Cat has been around for years."

"Point to you." Lisa sighed. "What do you need me to do? What are *we* going to do?"

Sawyer hadn't figured that out yet.

Chapter Eight

After a short call to Ephraim, Blake had the name and address of someone local who could get IDs for him and Reagan. He was happy to realize the contact was an old friend. A little while later, she parked in the rear parking lot of the photography studio he directed her to.

She shut off the engine and settled in her seat. "I saw a local bookstore a few blocks away. I'll be there when you're done."

"You have to go in with me." If every step a battle, accompanying her was a bad idea. That didn't mean he was going to take back the decision. Sucker for punishment, or something.

"I don't know this person, and I haven't had the best experience with your colleagues in the past," she said.

That was fair. He shoved down his impatience, to keep it from creeping into his voice. "This guy is from my pre-Hatter, pre-NSA days. We served together."

"Good. Catch up. Enjoy the reunion. Come find me when you're done." She rolled her head to look at him. "Unless you think I'm going to run. Are you going to handcuff me to the door?"

"We'll wait until we've been around each other at least a few more days before I explore this handcuff fixation of yours." He kept his tone light, rather than surrender to irritation. "If we're doing this together, you need to give me at least a little breathing-room, trust-wise."

"It's your associates I have concerns about. You've got leeway."

For someone so intelligent, she was a bit dim sometimes. "We're having IDs made, and that means we need a photo of you. My associate doesn't care who you are."

She opened her mouth, then snapped it shut again with a scowl.

"You can keep the taser while we're in there, if that helps you feel better. And you can linger someplace it's easy to bolt from except when he takes your picture."

"All right." She undid her seatbelt, climbed from the car, and walked with him through the front door. "Wow." She looked around the lobby. "It's *actually* a photography studio."

"A high-end one, just like the sign out front implies. Why does that surprise you?"

She jammed her hands into her pockets. "I don't know. I expected a pawnshop or a greasy spoon, or something low key and run down."

"You watch too much TV." Blake nodded toward the front desk. "Besides, this is the last place someone will look for a person who's making IDs with shitty photos on them."

The receptionist was watching them, brows raised. If Reagan and Blake hovered in the doorway much longer, it was going to get awkward.

"You mean I won't get a stunning glamour shot for this badge?" Reagan's pout was exaggerated.

"I'm sure you'll be stunning no matter what, but no, this will be the same as any other crappy, official identification." He rested a hand on the small of her back and guided her past the lobby.

Blake turned a wide smile on the girl behind the desk. "Afternoon. I'm Lance. Is Theo in?"

"One moment." The receptionist dialed her phone, then spoke into her headset. "There's a Lance here to see you. Of course." She disconnected and looked at Blake. "Go on up. Second floor, last door on the left at the end of the hall."

"Thanks."

Blake glanced at Reagan as she headed up the stairs. She looked back, brows raised, and smirk on her lips.

"What?" he asked.

"*Lance*? Really?" She kept her voice low.

"And?"

"As in, *Lance Corporal Allen*?"

It was his rank as a Marine. Since he was expected, it was the easiest way to indicate it was him, without giving up his real name. He shrugged. "As in."

She shook her head. "No wonder you're incapable of keeping a low profile."

He didn't have a comeback for that, but they'd reached Theo's office. Blake knocked.

"Come." The voice carried from inside.

Blake stepped into the room, and his grinned when he saw his old friend on the other side of the desk.

Theo returned the smile, and stepped forward to shake his hand and clap him on the shoulder. "Rumor was you bit it, working as a double agent."

"You know how rumors work," Blake said.

Theo looked past him at Reagan, who still lingered near the office entrance. "Ephraim told me what you wanted. He also said I should ask you why you're not on a plane to Fiji. Do I want to know what that means?" He dragged his gaze back to Blake.

"You really don't. But it's because I didn't get the answer to my question yet." Which wasn't true and wasn't supposed to be a factor in Blake's sticking around. "We need to be locals for the next twelve hours or so." He didn't need to elaborate. Theo would understand he meant local cops.

"One for each of you?"

"Please."

Theo pointed toward the door they'd come in through. "I'll need your photos. Step across the hall for that, and then give me half an hour."

Reagan protested when she saw the camera was digital. She didn't want her photo stored. Theo pointed out that was the only way to create the ID so it passed all appropriate checks.

"Besides," he said. "In about twelve hours, I have to erase all traces of these from the sheriff's database. The last thing you need is someone who knows the staff stumbling on them and wondering who the fuck you are. I'm only giving you that long, to ensure you're through all security checkpoints before I wipe the cards and you burn them."

"I'm good with that." Reagan seemed to relax.

Blake wasn't as comforted.

"You can wait in here, and I'll come get you when you're set." Theo led them to a metal, full-height cabinet at the back of his office, and pressed his thumb to a spot in back. The panel slid open without a sound.

Blake stepped aside for Reagan, then followed her into a small room with a couple of chairs, a table, and a mini fridge. She wore a tiny smile as she settled into a plastic seat.

"You spent the last half-hour bitching, and now you're amused?" Blake teased.

"It's not Narnia, but I'd be disappointed if there wasn't at least a little secret-agent subterfuge-type stuff going on. Room hidden behind a secret door? This gives me my fix." And there was another glimpse of not-so-jaded Reagan.

He chuckled. "I don't have an argument for that." He took the other free chair and leaned in to rest his arms on the table.

"Of course you don't, because it's a valid point."

Silence settled between them, not as comfortable as what he was used to with her. Not that there was much history to have an expectation of normalcy, but he did.

She drummed her fingers on the table. Blew a strand of hair out of her eyes. Settled her chin in her palms.

It was odd to think this was the same woman

who negotiated them the chance to walk away from a crime lord. Who, a few hours ago, stared down someone pointing a gun at her and didn't flinch. Who was bitter enough to mean it when she said she wanted to watch Jabberwock's empire burn.

Maybe she was in a better frame of mind now, to give him more details. "This trail we're following— Where did you get the information?"

"I told you. Alex."

Not the kind of detail he had in mind. "He's sending you notes from beyond the grave?"

"As far as you're concerned." Despite the retort, her voice didn't hold the edge it had earlier.

"As far as I'm concerned, six months ago you didn't even realize how deep he was in Wonderland. Now you have a path to deconstruct the entire thing, courtesy of him? I have to take a little leap of faith to go along with this, but really?"

She sighed and slumped in her chair. "You don't have to go with me." The immature response was an odd contrast to the situation.

"And you didn't have to accept my offer to help." He forced himself to adopt a less argumentative tone. "I get it; we don't trust each other. But something has to give here, for things to work. Do you think I'm still working for my former employers?"

"No." There was no hesitation in her response.

"Then who am I going to tell? Did Alex leave some sort of diary behind? That doesn't really scream *top secret.*"

"He left me a secret code that only I can figure

out."

Interesting. "How does that work?"

Her laugh was dry and humorless. "It would have worked a lot better if I'd figured it out a year ago. Before he died, Alex sent me a bunch of photos. It took me a long time to look at them, because… bad memories." She drew in a shaky breath and sniffled. "I should back up. When I was a kid, I loved puzzles."

"You? Nah." Blake winked.

She quirked her mouth in a half-smile. "It's true. I swear. Alex used to make up secret codes, to trip me up. When I cracked his code, he'd buy me an ice-cream sandwich. I would have made Pavlov proud—I'd practically drool each time Alex brought me a new riddle, partly for the sweets but mostly the challenge." Her voice drifted, as if following her into the memories she shared with Blake.

The combination of wistfulness and admiration on her face it made it painfully clear how much she cared about her brother. It helped give Blake a better insight into what set her on this path. "So he left you a code somehow? In the photos? Gang signs or something?"

"Image tags. Harmless shit most people wouldn't look twice at, but each image and its keywords has a new address or other piece of information in it."

"Why did it take you so long to see it?" Blake winced at the way the question emerged. "I didn't mean it like that."

"You did, and it's a fair question. I didn't know there was anything to look for. I thought Alex was a grunt, subject to the whims of the man up top. Then Jabberwock made the comment about Alex stashing money for my education, and it made me wonder what I'd missed."

Blake saw one big, glaring hole in the situation. "If Jabberwock sent you down this path and gave you the photos in question, how do you know he's not setting you up?"

"I don't. Not for certain." Frustration crept into her voice. "But the code… It's so much like what Alex did for me, and I discovered a journal written in his handwriting, and some of the other information I've found… I might have missed some things about my brother's lifestyle, but there are other things I know that he wouldn't have told almost anyone else. So I believe they're from him."

Blake had his doubts, but if it was Jabberwock leading them, it would be interesting to see the results. He just hoped Reagan wasn't chasing a ghost.

Chapter Nine

Sawyer had a rare few hours free to himself. Lisa stepped out to handle business, and he didn't have anything scheduled until this evening.

It would give him the time he needed to examine the Alice situation more closely. Seeing her again twice in such rapid succession had his blood racing. The meeting in Las Vegas, the single trespass on his servers, and then leading him to Salt Lake… What was she up to?

He navigated the directory structure on his laptop and brought up her folder. He recorded all of his interactions, no matter who they were with. Audio when that was the only option—thank God for cell phones with good mics—and video when he could.

It was insurance. Blackmail. Extortion. The term used depended on which side of the fence a person sat on.

Alice's videos had their own directory. The time she spent in his condo was disappointing, footage-wise, but he wasn't surprised. She must have known by then that most of what she did was monitored. She wasn't stupid. Not like most people.

He rarely replayed his recordings. He knew what each contained, and that was enough. Once in a while, he needed to confirm a detail. Listen to a tone of voice. See if someone had given more information than they intended to.

For the most part, however, people were rote and predictable. Emotional and melodramatic. It grated on his nerves to hear them a second time, if they hadn't offered anything of use the first. He didn't understand how they got worked up over insignificant things.

Lisa wasn't like that. She was cool. Removed. Blake hadn't been like that either. Until he met Alice. Which was unfortunate for Blake, because Alice wasn't the kind of person to get emotionally attached *just because*. She was an observer. She wasn't one of the people; she kept herself distant from them.

That was part of the reason he kept going back to her recordings. Especially the videos. She was on a different level than the average schmuck.

He knew exactly where the footage he sought was. It was from the day he took her clothes shopping. He'd watched the video of her in the dressing room a dozen times, but it never got old seeing her yield to his touch. Watching how she surrendered to his command, without losing herself.

He clicked *Play* and let the clip run again. It overlapped with his memories of what it was like to taste her. To make her moan. To see her kneel and take him in her mouth, but raise herself back to equal footing after.

Sawyer stroked his cock through his sweat shorts as he watched. Caressing his shaft. Sinking into reminiscing, as if she were here.

You don't have time for this. The thought disrupted his enjoyment. It was true, though. He had work to do. He could save indulging fantasies for the next time he encountered Alice.

Which would be under his terms, once he figured out what was going on in her head.

Blake and Reagan strolled through the airport, toward the security checkpoint. He glanced at her, his experience working with other people telling him she'd be on edge. But there was no hesitation in her step.

Perfect. If she kept her cool, and he did the same, they'd be on the plane in a few minutes, like he promised.

They approached the agent standing to the side of the metal detectors, and Blake flashed her a smile. He was reaching his fake-friendliness quota for the day. He handed over the badge Theo gave him. "Evening."

She barely glanced at him. "Where you heading?"

"Charlotte," Reagan said. She'd refused to fly directly into her destination airport, and he didn't blame her. "Picking up an extradition."

"Lucky bastard, if he doesn't have to take the bus." The agent looked between the badge and Blake, a frown sliding in.

Every muscle in his body tensed. Was there a

problem with their badges? No. Theo knew his shit. Out of the corner of his eye, he saw Reagan drop her hand to where she wore her taser.

Don't be stupid. He didn't know if he was willing the thought at her or himself.

"Utah County Sheriff's office?" the agent said. "You know Greg Evans?"

"Sure. Great guy." Blake prayed it was an innocent question, and not some sort of *that's-not-a-real-person* trick.

"He's my husband." She looked at Reagan, brow furrowed. "Pretty sure he would have mentioned someone so young coming on staff."

Fuck. Blake ticked off a list of options in his head. Running would make things worse. Could he call in another favor? On fake IDs, unlikely. Would someone be able to trace them back to their old lives?

"I'm on loan from Price." Reagan plucked her badge out of the agent's hands and pocketed it. "This guy screwed with a few sorority sisters, and I had to beg my boss to let me do this, but you see things like that…" She shuddered. "I'm sorry. It's hard for me to talk about, you know?"

"I hear you, hon." She handed back Blake's card as well. "If you happened to turn your head long enough for your partner to kick the guy in the balls…"

Blake chuckled. "I'll see what I can do. Thanks for your help."

He and Reagan resumed their stroll toward their departure gate, and it took the last of his restraint to keep a steady pace and look casual. They made it through. But what about next time?

Chapter Ten

The masks that the guests of the masquerade wore only hid a portion of their faces; most of the people were easily identifiable. Sawyer suspected there was a metaphor in there, about how people hid their true selves.

Not that most people had much to hide. Superficial creatures with petty concerns.

It didn't matter that only Nashville's wealthiest were invited to this affair; he did a visual inventory of everyone in the room. Lisa, her hand hooked through his arm, would do the same. They meandered from one pack of people to the next, shaking hands with women in satin dresses, whose necks were adorned with jewelry worth more than houses. They paused to chat with gentlemen in silk suits tailored for tonight, never to be worn again.

He never introduced himself or Lisa. A whisper ran through the room, waltzing with the string quartet seated near one wall. *Is that Jabberwock?*

"Pleased with yourself?" Lisa's question was so quiet, meant only for his ears. She'd opted for a red dress and wore a tiara. If a chess piece could come to life, she'd done it.

He patted her gloved hand. "Absolutely, my dear." His *costume* was more subtle. A suit that looked similar to everyone else's and a Phantom of the Opera half-mask. This evening, Jabberwock and Queen's appearance was a subtle power play. There were enough affluent people attending that the few who knew his face would whisper to those who didn't yet. They'd wonder why he was here. Who he was meeting with. What he wanted.

His gaze fell on a woman near the bar, swathed in blue that hugged her curves, matched her eyes, and ended above the knee. *Alice.* He paused, watching her move. The quirk of her lips when she laughed… Her pale skin against her sapphire dress…

"What are you—? Oh." Lisa's tone fell flat. "I suppose your plans for the evening have changed."

"At least for one dance." Sawyer knew Alice and Blake flew into Charlotte four days ago. He assumed they'd pop up in his part of the world soon, but he couldn't guess where or when. Alice was brilliant. Crafty. Fuck—he wanted to get inside her head and dismantle it, to see why she ticked differently than everyone else.

He hadn't figured they would be here, because they had to know someone, to get in. Then again, Blake knew people. And that bastard had the nerve to wear a top hat, with a tag tucked into the band that read 10/6.

Sawyer turned from the couple and toward another group of people. "We should mingle a little more."

"You're not going to say *hello* to Ms. Alice?" Lisa asked, voice infused with sarcasm and shock.

"She'll wait." He'd rather walk straight over there, to spend the rest of the party delving into Alice's head, twisting and turning and playing and fucking around, until he discovered what secrets she had to reveal. He wasn't finished with his priority here, though, and she wasn't going anywhere. After all, she was here to see him.

They approached a State senator, whose eyes grew wide when he recognized Sawyer. Few words were exchanged—a quick greeting and some generic talk about the weather—before Sawyer and Lisa moved on. They flitted around couples dancing, and traded smiles with someone he didn't recognize.

His gaze drifted back to Alice and the way the soft lighting teased the diamonds in her earrings. She looked at him, and the corner of her mouth quirked up in a half-smile before she turned back to Blake.

"Fuck mingling." Sawyer turned back toward Lisa. "How would you like to catch up with an old acquaintance?"

"You have zero staying power. Does your obsession realize that?"

Sawyer flashed Lisa a smile, his eyes narrowed. "Keep Blake company for me."

"I'd love to."

He wasn't sure if that was dry sarcasm or simply a lack of enthusiasm on her part.

As they approached, Alice looked up, mischief sparkling in her eyes from behind her mask, and Blake glanced up from his drink for the briefest moment before returning his attention to the amber liquid. Sawyer didn't think for a second that meant Blake wasn't paying attention to everything.

Sawyer extended his hand toward Alice. "Dance with me?"

Blake tightened his jaw, and his knuckles grew so pale Sawyer was surprised the glass didn't shatter in his grip.

"I'd love to." Alice fit her palm against Sawyer's and let him lead her to the center of the room, with the other couples enjoying the sonata.

She looked like she belonged here, from the confidence with which she held herself, to the way she slid into his arms without hesitation and rested a hand on his shoulder. And—fuck—her body fit against his like she was made for him.

Most people had habits he didn't understand. Overreacted to the tiniest stimulus. Alice wasn't like that. She had a cool, removed perspective. She still slipped up. Let the wrong things get to her. But she would learn, and he'd help.

He adopted a dance step that kept time with the music, leading her across the pale swirls in the rug. "I didn't expect to see you so soon," he said. "Not that I'm complaining."

"I couldn't stay away." Her voice was light and casual. Comfortable and assured, like when he spoke with her in the casino, nothing like that of the out-of-place girl he rescued in a church parking lot.

"But you brought a friend."

"*Brought* makes it sound like he's part of my plan. He's not."

Sawyer spun them as the tune hit a crescendo then dialed back. The faint scent of something playful—cherries or bubblegum maybe—drifted from her, mingling with the aroma of the fresh flowers dotted in vases around the room. He dipped his head to draw his nose along the side of her neck, and she whimpered.

"Why would I believe that?" he murmured against the smooth curve of her shoulder.

She tilted her head, allowing him easier access. "Because you've been watching him, and I haven't been with him almost since I walked away from you."

"I suspect the two of you haven't been together; I don't *know* it. I don't watch him twenty-four-seven." He was tired of talking about Blake. He wanted to spend more time focused on the beauty in his arms. "You, on the other hand… I could spend hours studying you. We could start with you stripping off that dress and showing me what you learned while we were apart."

"Speaking of…" The smooth, flirty seduction never in her tone never wavered. "What are you up to these days?"

Another couple danced closer, and Alice pressed into Sawyer. Her heat seared him through his suit, as if there were no clothing between them, making him wish that were the case. He traced his fingers down her spine, and she arched her back with a light laugh, which brought her even nearer.

"I'm looking for a cat," he said.

As they twirled, she put an extra step between them and looked at him, brows raised. "You're better than that. A pussy joke?"

A few feet away, the commissioner's aide

glared at her at the word *pussy*. Sawyer swallowed a laugh. The man would be fucking his boss's wife later tonight, which meant he had zero right to judge.

Sawyer shook his head. "It's not, but if you're offering, I won't turn down the distraction."

"I don't remember offering."

"No?" He tightened his grip on her waist, closing the distance between them. "Look at all these people," he whispered in her ear, "hiding their ugliness, their desires, and their perversions. Not under their masquerade mask, but behind the face they wear every time they talk to someone else. What do you think they'd do, if I lifted you onto a table, pushed your dress up to your hips, and fucked you right now?"

Alice's breathing quickened, her chest pressing into his. "If there are any fans of the dressmaker in the room, they'd gasp when you tore the satin."

He nipped her earlobe. "You're avoiding my question."

"You're hoping I'll say something like, *They'd watch*?" She licked flushed, full lips.

He wanted to do that for her. Nibble on that half-pout until she groaned. "I was hoping you'd say, *Freak the fuck out and start spewing moral bullshit they don't believe*, but your answer is better. Are you up for helping me give them a show?"

"No."

"But you're picturing us doing it anyway." He was. Talk about Jabberwock leaving an impression.

He wasn't fooling anyone. It wasn't the idea

of having an audience that made him hard; it was the memory of her lips wrapped around his cock.

"I am," she said.

Fuck. Her answer made his erection ache. "Do you miss it? The sex? Do you ever lie alone in bed, stripped naked, running your hands over your body while you think about that night in the VR club? Do you finger yourself to orgasm, diving into the fantasy of what it would have felt like to let me keep going, with half that room watching us?"

"No. But I appreciate the inspiration."

"What would you say if I told you I don't believe you?"

"I'd say I expect to hear that from you a lot, over the next couple of months." She stepped away from him again, to look him in the eye. "I'm starting to think you only see me as a toy."

He feigned shock and hurt. "*Never*. You're much more fun than that. You didn't break when I played with you too hard." And that was one of the things that fascinated him about her the most. She was drawn to his darkness, but something held her back from diving in head first. Indoctrination? Possibly. Blake? Likely.

It didn't matter. Sawyer would figure out how to teach Alice what she was missing out on.

The sonata reached its final refrain, then ended. Alice dropped her hand and pulled from his embrace. "My date is waiting."

"He's got company. You can stay for one more dance." Sawyer grabbed her wrist and pulled her back to him.

She looked at him, eyes wide with fear and

desire. "Yes, sir."

Why weren't they someplace more private? He had another song; he could coax her into a dark corner by the end of it.

Blake should be watching the room, but he struggled to pull his gaze from Reagan and Jabberwock. The only other time he'd seen them together, she'd been a deer frozen in the headlights.

Tonight, she slid into the role of Jabberwock's dance partner without hesitation. They looked good together, if Blake shoved aside his loathing for Jabberwock. It was disconcerting to watch Reagan seduce another man.

Is she doing the same to you?

No. This was the game. He played a part for years; it didn't make him Hatter. A fist clenched around Blake's heart, and he had to force himself to tell the bartender he didn't need another drink. He needed his wits about him tonight.

Queen—it was odd to call her something besides *Dormouse*—sat on the stool next to him, on her phone. The organization required work at odd hours. His, *How's business?* died in his throat. He wasn't interested in those details, even if she was willing to share them.

"They're still dancing?" She dropped her

digital leash in her handbag and turned to him. She looked Blake over. "Lap dog doesn't suit you."

He snorted. "You're one to talk. Still on his arm. You're not a decoration."

"You're right. I'm not." She waved the bartender over and said, "Sparkling water with a wedge of lime. Skip the lime for my companion." Queen looked at Blake again. "He and I are equal partners. Do you prefer your new life?"

"Not answering to the whims of a psychopath? Yes. I prefer this." Despite the tension flowing between them—so thick he could slice it with the blade she kept hidden on her hip, inside the intricate folds of her skirt—this was familiar from the fact she knew what he drank, to the stilted conversation.

She shrugged. "To each their own. I'm sorry about what happened at the diner."

"It caught me off guard, that's for sure. Have the rules about not opening fire in public places changed?" He twirled the little black straw in his glass, his attention drifting back to Reagan, on the dance floor.

"No. Knave had a hard-on for you, because… I actually couldn't tell you. But he's been dealt with."

"Glad to hear it." He wasn't really grateful for the news; he never liked the loss of life that came with Hatter's position. "Water under the bridge, then."

Queen followed his gaze to Jabberwock and Reagan, then looked at Blake again. "How goes the quest to burn our empire to the ground? Her behavior makes me wonder if she knows what that means."

"Honestly? I couldn't tell you. I'm just a lapdog, remember?"

"Touché. Are you at least enjoying the lap?"

"Immensely." It was a half-truth. Closer to reality than most of their conversation, but still a deception. He and Reagan were staying in the same hotel room but hadn't slept together—or more—since they hooked up in Salt Lake. She'd put up an effective wall, blocking him every time he tried to dig into any conversation outside of discussing tonight.

A loud *bang* shattered the room when every door slammed shut at once. "*Everyone down on the floor,*" a man at the front of the room shouted. "We're here to relieve you of your accessories."

Cliché much? Blake wanted to kick himself for not noticing the men skulking near the exits sooner. Six total, two by each door, wearing full masks and cheap suits, and wielding assault rifles.

Screams and shouts rippled through the partygoers, as some scrambled under tables and others ran into each other in an attempt to get away.

Blake drew his gun and leveled it at the armed man nearest him. He didn't have to look, to know Queen did the same. Instinct flowed whispered through him with memories of the past.

Jabberwock drew on the two near the third exit. "You gentlemen are making a mistake, but there's still time to leave."

The gunman who had shouted didn't flinch. Eardrum shattering shots overlaid terrified yells when he opened fire on the room, hosing down the walls with bullets. He hit a vase, sending glass, water, and shards of flower flying. "I *said* down on the ground. You three. Guns to me."

Unpredictable and not afraid to open fire. This required a subtler approach. Blake and Queen joined the rest of the guests in lying on the ground, after they both tossed their weapons aside.

Jabberwock pulled Reagan to him, half covering her with his frame as they assumed similar prone positions. Blake clenched his jaw. The protective gesture cut a deeper gash than the flirting had.

Adrenaline filled him with ice. If this went on much longer, he'd lose his chance at surprise.

Reagan's whimper cut through the bedlam. Blake's heart cracked, but another feeling rolled along his racing pulse. A compulsion he didn't have the focus to put a name to.

A gunman whirled on her and leveled his rifle at her head. "Shut the fuck up."

"She's scared, man." Jabberwock's voice was even. "Give her a break."

It was enough of an exchange to draw the attention of the thief's partners. As most everyone else in the room turned to watch, Blake shared a glance with Queen. It took a blink from her—that millisecond of recognition—and he grabbed the pistol strapped to his ankle.

They stood at the same time, spinning in different directions, and he heard her two gunshots overlap his. Jabberwock's gunfire added a third track to the chorus, and a heartbeat later, six gunmen lay dead on the floor.

Chaos erupted in the room, panic amplified

as the herd stampeded.

Queen looked at Blake. "How about that? You have yourself a damsel in distress."

He doubted Reagan's reaction was any more real than her enjoyment of Jabberwock's company. "No. I really don't." The banter and actions were too easy to fall into. Too familiar. They mingled with recollections of working side by side with Dormouse and Hare. The three had good chemistry when work required it. Blake wasn't sure which terrified him more—the ease with which he slid into being the third, or that Reagan filled a space in the equation, as if it had been left for her. "Exit strategy?"

"South door. There's a car waiting." Queen headed in that direction. She discarded her sidearm, and he followed suit but grabbed his original piece from the ground. He wasn't joining her unarmed, but he was going with her. Jabberwock would bring Reagan to the same place. She and Blake had a far better chance of walking away from this with their current company than alone. If Queen wanted them dead, she could have executed him then Reagan amid the mayhem.

The rest of the details would come when they weren't in the middle of a war zone.

The guests cut a wide path when Blake and Queen moved toward the exit. A woman stepped in the blood seeping into the carpet, and squealed as Blake passed. His eardrums were going to be ringing for days.

When they stepped outside, a large black sedan was waiting, as Queen said it would be.

Jabberwock held the door for Reagan, then

slid in next to her and wrapped an arm around her waist. Blake bit his tongue—he didn't have a claim to her—but fuck if he didn't want to deck the other man and pull her back to his side.

He settled for gesturing to the row of seats that faced theirs, and telling Queen, "After you."

She gave him a curt nod, a smile playing on her lips. "Thank you." She had her phone out.

The car pulled onto a back road, and sirens faded in the background as the driver took them away from the scene of the bedlam.

"Are you all right?" Blake asked Reagan.

She sat with her back rigid and a matching expression. She looked like ice, the way her blue dress contrasted with her pale skin. "I'm fine."

He wanted to push, but this wasn't the place or the company. Six months ago, it was easy to leave the posh part of this job behind. Tonight, it was just as simple to slide back into the role of one of Jabberwock's executioners.

He shoved aside questions of what that said about him, and looked at Jabberwock. "There was a time when rumors of our presence guaranteed an evening would go smoothly."

"*Our*?" Jabberwock pursed his lips.

"It's not as though every thug in town knows who or where he is." Reagan scooted on her seat, putting a few inches between her and Jabberwock.

Her action contradicted the way she jumped to his defense, and Blake ground his teeth.

Queen looked up. "This wasn't coincidence." She looked at Reagan, eyes narrowed, then turned to her boss.

"Cat?" Jabberwock asked.

Queen nodded. "That's the word…"

"You were serious earlier." Reagan sounded surprised. It was the first real emotion she'd shown since climbing in the car.

"Deadly serious." Jabberwock smirked, as if he'd made a brilliant joke.

Blake swam through the vague comments, to put puzzle pieces together. "*Cat*, as in *Cheshire*? But—"

"He's not real," Jabberwock said. "Sound like anyone else you know? Me, for instance?"

Blake didn't see the similarities. "He's *actually* not real. There's no evidence he even has an organization."

"Until recently." Reagan twisted in her seat and looked between the three.

"And you know that how?" Queen asked.

Blake wondered the same thing.

"If I'm going to dismantle what you've created, I have to know your competition." Reagan sounded like the answer was obvious.

Queen rolled her eyes. "Lovely. Where can we drop the two of you?"

"Down, girl." Jabberwock patted her knee.

"You don't already know?" Blake asked.

Queen gave him a thin smile. "I do. But it's polite to ask."

Blake was grateful to call it a night. Put as much distance between Hatter, Hare, and Dormouse as possible, before more of why he enjoyed his former job rushed back to mock him.

Chapter Twelve

Blake had to focus, to keep his hand from shaking with excess energy as he unlocked their hotel room door. He pushed it open and stepped aside for Reagan. She hadn't said anything since they climbed from the car a few minutes ago, and now she brushed past him without a word.

He needed to burn off the rush, building—

The bathroom door slammed, and a second later, the sound of retching obliterated his thoughts. He couldn't ignore his relief that she wasn't shrugging off the evening, but he winced in sympathy with each new heave.

When the sounds stopped, he tried the handle and found it unlocked. "Reagan?" he called through the door. "I'm coming in."

"'Kay." Her voice was tired.

He stepped into the bathroom, to find her sitting next to the toilet, legs tucked to the side and bound by her dress, and head in her hands over the porcelain. His gut lurched at the smell of bile mixed with disinfectant.

"Don't move." He filled a glass with water

from the tap, and handed it to her. "Slow sips."

"I know how puking works. Thanks." She took the drink from him and rinsed her mouth out. Mascara smudged her face, and her cheeks were splotched with red.

He got a washcloth damp, then knelt next to her and tucked a few flyaway strands of hair behind her ears before running the cool terrycloth over her skin.

"You must think I'm completely inept, losing my shit as soon as we walked in the door." She let out a bitter laugh. "The poor little girl who needs saving all the time."

It was startling but reassuring to see the contrast between the woman who fake-freaked-out at the masquerade, and this genuine girl who had seen too much, and couldn't always mask her reactions.

"There's a part of me that likes the notion of being your white knight." He meant the words to be playful and teasing, but their truth sank like a stone in his chest. "I don't have any illusions that you'd be lost without me, though." He wanted to. There was a bit of him—and not a small bit, either—infatuated with the idea only he could save this girl. But each time he was arrogant enough to think along those lines, she proved him wrong.

She leaned against the washcloth, resting her weight on his hand. "At the party, the three of you didn't hesitate. Not for a second. There wasn't any of that drawn-out talking I've seen in movies, or with Jabberwock when he's gloating. Tonight..." She shuddered and pulled away, wrapping her arms around herself. "Never mind. I should get cleaned up."

He traced a thumb along her face, pulling her gaze to his. "I'll be in the other room. We'll talk when you're done."

"I don't need to talk."

He disagreed, but the bathroom floor wasn't the place to convince her otherwise. "I'll be in the other room," he repeated.

He settled on the couch, in front of the TV. They were staying in a hotel room nicer than any apartment he'd lived in during his pre-Hatter days. It was part of the airs they'd put on for the party. Rich, affluent couple from out of town, here to mingle with the local money. Everything was glass and brushed steel and sleek.

He grabbed the remote but didn't hit *On*. Sitting still ached—it cramped in his muscles and made him grind his teeth—but the fewer excuses Reagan had to ignore him, the better. He stripped off his jacket and draped it over the arm of the couch. His bowtie followed.

Several minutes passed before she emerged, face red but no longer splotchy, and hair tied back from her face in a simple ponytail. She sat next to him, close enough her heat teased him without her making contact.

"What are you watching?" Her voice was flat. A glance told him wrinkles marred her dress now, and a rip ran up the right leg, almost to the thigh.

"A documentary on ink. They're doing black right now."

She gave a dry chuckle. "Looks fascinating."

They sat in silence, staring at the powered-off

screen. He was afraid, if he pushed too hard, she'd vanish into the bedroom, or worse, dive into a distraction.

The excess adrenaline pumping inside screamed *yes* at that idea. Sex wouldn't fix much, but it sure would burn away the tension for a few hours. He forced the thought aside.

"When I was in that cell, and they ran those videos non-stop, I thought I'd become desensitized to some things." Reagan's voice was quiet, mingling with the white noise in the room. "You know what they showed me, don't you?"

"I do." Mostly gruesome photos of deaths tied back to Jabberwock.

"You're a killer. You try and hide it under excuses and being the good guy, but it's part of you. Tonight, you shot without hesitation—and thank God, because someone has to act, right? I've accepted that you have a past that would chew me up from the inside out if I'd lived it. All three of you…" She hugged herself. "But knowing it and seeing it are two different things, and there was so much blood and glass and flower petals mixed with dark-red splatter, and I can't get those images out of my head, and—"

"Stop." When he shifted to face her, leather creaked under him. "You can't fall into this. It's not the kind of thing you can block out, and yes, you'll have to deal with it, but if you let yourself drown in it, you'll never climb back out."

She scrubbed her face. "What am I supposed to do?"

"Focus on something else for a little while."

"I can still feel his hands on my waist. My hand. My back." Reagan stared ahead, expression pinched and voice strained.

This wasn't working, and she was worrying him. Blake stood and tugged her to her feet. "Come on." He led her toward the bedroom.

She stopped several feet short of the door and jerked her hand from his. "I'm not up for this."

"What?" He spun to face her, and her meaning sank in. "I'm not… This isn't about sex."

"What is it, then?"

"You need to remove yourself from the world. We're going to hide in there and talk about whatever you want, as long as it's not tonight. I do recommend you change, for comfort's sake, but if you'd rather keep the dress on, you can."

"I'd really rather not. I don't think I ever want to see it again."

He gestured toward the room, and she stepped inside ahead of him. As he joined her, he removed his shoulder holster and set it on the nightstand.

"Unzip me?" Her quiet request was a gunshot against his humming nerves.

He turned to see her standing with her back to him. "Of course." He dragged the zipper down, and the satin fell aside, exposing her skin. His libido roared for him to kiss down her spine, but he beat back the impulse. If she didn't want that kind of intimacy, he could push his base instincts aside.

She shrugged the dress off, and it slid to the ground where it pooled in a swathe of fabric at her feet. She pulled on the T-shirt she held, before she turned to face him.

"This is about comfort, huh?" She focused her gaze on her fingers as she undid the buttons on his shirt one at a time. Her expression, lips pursed and brows furrowed, made it look like the act took all her concentration.

She pushed his top off, then reached to untuck his undershirt. Her nails scraped his skin, and he sucked in a sucked in a sharp breath through his teeth.

Reagan traced the scars on his left shoulder. A fist clenched around his chest, though he couldn't feel her touch. It was the cluster where he was shot, when he was in the Marines. The wound that got him discharged.

With a feather-light touch, she followed an invisible line down his arm, to the tattoo on his bicep.

"You've seen those before," he said.

"That was different. Now they feel more… real. Story of my life. I swear each new day is another thing I thought I understood until I lived it. It's all too real…" She looked up, past him rather than at him.

If he looked over his shoulder, he wouldn't see what she was looking at. He'd worn that same haunted expression too many times.

Her light kiss—a whisper of lips on lips— caught him off-guard.

"We're getting comfortable. I'm pretty sure you said that," she said.

He pointed her at the bed. "I did." A flash from the party blinked through his thoughts. The flirting with Jabberwock. The whimper when the gunmen showed up. How much of that was show? Was he being played here?

No one was this good an actor. He settled on the mattress next to Reagan, his back against the headboard.

She curled up next to him, head against his shoulder. "You don't have to sleep in the other room. Tonight or any night."

He did. "This is the exception. We both know it's better we don't make a habit of this."

"I guess." She slid down his torso until her head lay on his leg. Her blonde locks spread out over the dark of his slacks, and he could couldn't help trailing his fingers through the tresses. She let out a tiny sigh and nestled closer.

He wasn't sure how much time passed, neither of them speaking. He didn't want to twist, to look at the clock, and risk disturbing her. Her breathing evened and slowed.

He sat there until his leg fell asleep. Move and risk waking her up, or stay a little longer? It wasn't all about her. There was something soothing about being closed off from the rest of the world this way.

She mewled, and his calm evaporated. When the sound grew louder, and she squirmed, he shook her shoulder. "Reagan." He kept his voice soft, not wanting to add to whatever dreams chased her. "Wake up."

She bolted straight up, eyes wide. As she focused on him, the terror on her face faded behind a mask of ice. Without a word, she rolled from the bed, grabbed a couple pills from a bottle in her bag, and swallowed them dry. "I'm up for the day." She plopped back next to him. The sweet confusion that lingered around her earlier was gone. "If you want to get some more sleep, the bed is yours."

What did she take? "Come on." He stood and shook the tingles from his leg, then stripped off his slacks. "Give it one more try."

"I'm good. Really."

"Are you going to not sleep the rest of the night? It's only eleven."

She sighed and rolled her eyes. "I guess I could try again, if you're staying."

"I am." He pulled back the covers and waited for her to climb under before joining her.

She lay with her back to him but grabbed his arm and draped it over her hip, snuggling against his chest.

As she relaxed under his touch, resting more of her weight against him, and her frame rising and falling in a slow, steady pattern, the tension ratcheting his neck eased. She'd drifted off again.

Sunlight hit Blake's face, jarring him awake. He frowned when he saw he was in an otherwise empty hotel bed, instead of on the couch. Then the night before rushed back. He was on his feet in an instant.

"Reagan?"

The bathroom door was wide open and the light off. Her bag was still here, and so was his sidearm, but her shoes were missing. She wasn't in the main room either. Where was she?

"Fuck."

Did she bolt in the middle of the night? Wait until he was out, then take the chance to leave? Why last night, rather than before?

He walked back to the bedroom and grabbed the bottle she'd fished out last night. It was white and opaque, no label. The pills inside were capsules, with no brand or other indicator of type on them.

"*Fuck.*"

Chapter Thirteen

A faint whir reached Blake, the latch on the door clicked and Reagan stepped into the room. A plastic shopping bag hung from one of her wrists, and she held two coffee cups.

She looked him up and down, gaze lingering on his crotch, and he remembered he only wore boxers. "Hey, sexy." Her light and playful tone would have been pleasant, if it weren't such a stark contrast to the night before. "Are you all right?"

"Fine." He wasn't going to admit he'd worked himself into a frenzy at the thought of her walking out on him again.

"Good." She handed him one of the cups, then set the bag on the table. "I couldn't sleep, so I went for a run. I bought muffins." She pulled several individually wrapped snacks out and set them in a line. "I wasn't sure what kind you liked, so I bought one or two of everything. And there was a note for us at the front desk." She plucked out a white envelope last.

The flap was torn at the corner, leaving it open. On the front, in neat, red script, it said *Mad*

Hatter and Alice. Blake didn't like the look of that. "What is it?"

"Her Majesty, Queen, has invited us to tea… at The Chess Board." Reagan handed him the note.

He *really* didn't like the sound of that. His phone rang before he could summon a reply, and he grabbed it. "Yeah."

"Do you remember that night in Phoenix?" Ephraim asked.

Blake's blood turned chilly in his veins at the terse lack of greeting. It was a code they'd learned years ago. "I can't say I do."

"Checkmate."

If Ephraim was calling, law enforcement knew where they were. Blake disconnected, and tossed his phone aside. He'd get a new one at the next stop. If it was being used to trace him, they already knew the device was here.

Reagan set her coffee down, expression going blank. "What is it?"

"We need to go *now*." He grabbed his gun from the bedroom, yanked on a pair of jeans and a T-shirt, tossed on a hoodie to hide his gun, and then hesitated.

Reagan waited near the door, tapping her toes.

"No argument?" he asked.

"You said *now*. I assumed you meant it. Are we leaving?" She reached for the handle.

"Yes."

They strolled together to the elevator, pace casual. Taking the stairs down twenty flights would make them look like they were hiding something.

This way, they were as bland as any other guest.

"Who are we running from?" Reagan asked as they stepped into a lift.

"Law enforcement. I don't know more than that, but if he called, he picked something up."

"Who's *he*?"

Blake didn't know if they had time to make it out the front door, but they didn't have much of a choice. If whoever it was had already arrived, they had all the exits covered, and leaving via something like the loading docks would draw far more attention than walking onto the main sidewalk, like a normal guest. "A friend I trust."

"That must be nice."

Blake would read more into her tone and meaning later. Now, exit was the only objective.

Sawyer would rather be back home, in the war room, sifting through this nonsense with Lisa. Or seeking out Alice and puzzling through what was going on in her head. Lisa had a point; he might be a touch obsessed. Not that he saw that as a bad thing.

But the books had to be balanced, and accounts seen after, and a fresh wave of something loyalty- and fear-inducing, to go with his name. The affair with Cheshire Cat was costing him. He always figured he'd be the last person to be pissed off at a fictional character, but here it was.

An alert email pinged his phone, jarring him from his work. When he let Blake and Alice walk, then scrubbed them, he'd set up alerts on their legal names. It was for his own curiosity, to know if anyone saw past the work he'd done.

This alert was for Blake Allen—a common name, so Sawyer saw hundreds a week. This one had a picture with it, though. As well as a warrant and a national all-points bulletin.

Sawyer left his hotel room, walked the couple of feet to the one next door, and knocked.

The moment Lisa answered, he brushed past her. "We want to see this," he said as he snagged the remote from its spot near the TV and flipped to a news channel.

"What is *this*?"

He held up a finger to silence her. "If this is as big as I think, you'll see. Give it a few minutes."

Less than five minutes later, the anchor said, *"Federal law enforcement raided a hotel in Nashville, based on information that a known cyber terrorist, thought dead, was staying there. Blake Allen—"*

"Holy shit." Lisa sat on the edge of her bed. "We took them off the books. Faked their deaths. How did this happen?"

Their deaths had to be faked because people remembered a lot longer than federal databases did. Erasing someone from a computer didn't clear them from their colleagues' heads. But Sawyer wanted to know what resurrected Blake and Alice. "Perhaps someone who worked with him caught wind he was still out there."

The TV droned in the background. *"...suspect was gone when law enforcement arrived..."*

Lisa studied him. "Is *caught wind* your code

for *I tipped them off?*"

"God no. Having the Feds poking around will be incredibly disruptive. Alice just came out of hiding, and if she vanishes again, I have to reset the chessboard."

"That's not the most convincing argument. Do you realize that?" Lisa's gaze drifted back to the screen every few seconds.

Spoilsport. "Fine. How's this? If they're looking for him, they're going to want to discover how he vanished. That leads back to us. Not a headache we need on good days. Right now? It could be devastating." His irritation grew as he spoke. He shouldn't have to explain himself.

"Point made. If it wasn't you, who was it?"

"Alice." The other day when Lisa gave the answer off the cuff. Today, Sawyer understood where her assumption came from.

Lisa rolled her eyes. "She called law enforcement on herself?"

"But she didn't. They were gone with the cops showed up."

"Coincidence. It's ten in the morning; they went out to breakfast. Next you're going to tell me she hired those shitty excuses for thieves last night." Boredom leaked into Lisa's voice, and she turned off the news.

The more they talked this through, the more pieces fell into place. "The guys who never shot *at* anyone? They didn't have to know who she was, if they were hired to hit the party and remind me I wasn't untouchable."

"She was terrified when it was over." Lisa's

argument blended with her ho-hum. "There's no way you missed her shaking like a leaf."

He'd noticed. "She watched six men executed in quick succession. She's not a killer, and if she hired them… double the nausea that she got them killed. Are you trying to talk me out of this?"

"I'm asking you to see the holes in your logic. I said she was Cat as a joke. This is a conspiracy theory that defies even your reputation."

Which was why it was the perfect cover or distraction, or whatever one wanted to call it. "She's got it in her. Don't underestimate the woman."

"Not for a second." Lisa gave a short laugh and shook her head. "Someone who knows exactly when to whimper or fuck up when a gun is pointed at her, to get the response she needs? She knows how to play your strings and Blake's."

"So you agree with me." He didn't try to hide his smugness.

"I don't. If you're trying to convince me Alice is Cheshire Cat, you're as mad as a hatter." She gestured to the door. "Can I get back to work now?"

Sawyer clenched his jaw and bit back an angry retort. No reason to prove her right. It took more focus than he expected, to talk himself back from mounting rage.

Chapter Fourteen

As he and Reagan strolled away from the hotel, Blake forced himself to keep an even gait. They walked into the wind, to have an excuse to keep their heads down. The chill bit into his face, mocking him for the decision.

They needed to get someplace safe and assess the situation, but it was a Catch 22. Without knowing what the situation was, he had no idea where was safe, and he didn't dare call Ephraim, and put his friend in danger, until Blake had an idea what was going on.

He wrapped an arm around Reagan's waist, to pull her close. It would give the impression they were a couple walking the downtown streets.

She leaned into him without protest. "Where are we going?" Her question barely reached his ears over the November gusts.

"Not a clue. Closest bus stop, to start. We'll take a bus out of town, to the farthest stop that looks like it's got commerce." Because wandering a random suburban neighborhood without a destination was low on his list of things he wanted to do today. If a helpful member of a neighborhood-watch group decided Blake and Reagan looked suspicious, he didn't see any scenario where things ended well for them.

Conversation faded. He counted off each block, as they crossed the streets between. Four, then five. At this rate, they were going to walk out of town before they found a ride.

They turned the corner as an outbound bus pulled up to a bench about ten feet away. Reagan quickened her pace to match his, and a moment later they sat in the back. People occupied the seats around them, which meant talking would have to wait. That was fine; he didn't have enough information to say much.

When the vehicle rolled forward, a blast of humid, warm air hit him on the face. It smelled like feet and cigarette butts. He didn't care, as long as nobody was threatening them.

Reagan leaned her head on his shoulder, and he intertwined his fingers with hers. He didn't believe for a second it was anything other than for show.

They didn't talk, their ride taking them farther from the city center with each stop.

Reagan's body went rigid against his, and his senses kicked up another level. She knelt on her seat, and kissed along the edge of his ear. "Guy in front of me is watching news on his iPad," she whispered.

Blake clenched her hand more tightly but kept a lazy smile in place. "Anything interesting?"

She cupped his cheek, turning his head as if to kiss him, and pointed him in the direction of the screen. His heart plummeted into his shoes when he saw his own face staring back at him, courtesy of an old government ID. He couldn't make out the scrolling text beneath, but the larger headline banner read *Suspect wanted for questioning by the NSA*.

Fuck. He pulled the cord, to indicate they wanted to get off at the next stop, and before the bus finished rolling up to the bench, he tugged Reagan toward the rear exit.

They were only about ten miles out from where they started. They needed to put more distance between them and his former employer. She tucked herself next to his side as they stuck close to buildings and kept out of the flow of foot traffic.

"Were you able to see what else they were saying?" he asked.

"I caught some of the ticker news. They raided the hotel where they thought you were staying, and you were gone, so they're looking for you."

Shit. "Why are they looking for me now?" Jabberwock was supposed to take care of erasing them. Did Blake step on his toes in some way last night, to provoke this? Was it part of *the game*?

She shook her head.

"Is your name or picture up there?" He hadn't seen her, but he wasn't watching for long.

"Not that I could tell, but I only watched long enough to see you."

She may not be on their radar. If Jabberwock wanted her, this was a good way to get Blake out of the picture. Blake wasn't certain that was what happened, but odds seemed good. He steered them toward a convenience store. "I need you to buy me a pack of smokes."

"Because… stress relief?"

"Because I need to keep my head down, and stay away from places with cameras or TV's, if my face is plastered everywhere. If I'm lingering outside of every building we walk up to, I'm going to look like a creepy fucker, just standing outside hiding my face, unless I'm doing something."

Her chuckle was bitter. "The odd lump under your hoodie isn't doing you any favors."

"Cigarettes?"

"What kind?"

"Something light." He wasn't going to smoke them; he gave up that habit years ago.

She broke away from him, to head inside, and he took the opportunity to get a better idea of their surroundings. There was a diner on one corner, an auto shop down the street, and several businesses in between. When he looked in the other direction, he couldn't fight his relieved smile. A motel, complete with a sign whose cracks and chips he saw from here, and all of the single-story units with outside entrances.

Reagan returned, carrying a plastic bag. She handed him a box of Camel lights and held up the sack. "I figured, since we skipped breakfast…"

Inside were a few packages of nuts and a couple bottles of water. Smart woman. He nodded toward the motel. "Get us a room? We'll watch the news and see how bad this is, and figure out where to go next."

"Sounds like a plan."

Six hours later, sequestered in their room, Blake had watched the news shift from him being wanted for questioning, to the NSA having evidence he'd been in the hotel room they raided, to him being implicated in a shooting last night that left six people dead. His prints were the only ones identifiable on weapons found at the scene of the crime.

"I'm curious," he said, more to fill the air and distract himself, than because he wanted the answer. He sat on the edge of the bed, on the comforter. Part of him was afraid to pull the blanket back and reveal whatever lay underneath. The room was clean, but a layer of grime clung to everything anyway.

Reagan looked up from where she sat at the desk. "About what?"

"Jabberwock was supposed to erase us, correct? There were faked deaths. I know because I read about them. But *erasing* would also mean removing us from all law-enforcement databases."

"I assume. Or rather, that's what a rational person would do in a case like that." She had a point.

"If that's the case, what are they matching my fingerprints to?"

"Physical copies, instead of digital?" She turned her attention back to her phone.

Not likely, unless they dug through old records at Fort Knox or something, and there was no reason to do that unless they already suspected him. Something that shouldn't happen if they thought he was dead. He sifted the riddle through his head, but it didn't matter which angle he examined it from; he got the same answer each time. He wasn't as erased as he was supposed to be.

"Where does Alex say we're going next?" he asked. They needed a direction, and if Jabberwock was working this hard to take Blake out of the picture, they needed to head that way fast.

"It's a bit vague"—she swiped at her screen—"but the way I interpret it, Minnesota."

They'd need warmer clothes for that. "The way you interpret it?"

"He mentions street names and small suburbs. The problem is a lot of them are names like *Springfield*, where there's one in almost every state. This note says SD, Lakeville, WF, 270, and based on his previous notes, that means a safety deposit box at the Wells Fargo in Lakeville Minnesota, on 270th Street."

"Makes a hell of a lot more sense than most things I've heard today." Blake was great with any place that took them away from prying eyes.

"Got it." Reagan grinned and set her phone aside.

"Got what?"

"Kid about twenty-five miles from here, willing to sell his beater car for cash."

"*Suspect is considered armed and dangerous, and should not be approached. If you have any leads about this man, please contact the hotline immediately.*"

Blake glared at the TV. His ID photo stared back at him blankly. Working for Jabberwock and the NSA meant keeping his identity a secret was the key to staying alive. This was the first time since he left that he felt exposed without that guaranteed anonymity. "Great. When can you pick it up?"

Chapter Fifteen

Blake followed the worn path in the motel-room carpet as he paced. At least he wasn't the first person to take this route. Reagan was gone too long. Okay, it was only a couple hours, but all she had to do was take a cab to the guy selling the car, exchange money for keys, and come back here.

Even with a test drive and traffic building toward rush-hour levels, she should be done by now.

Whoever was bringing this head down on him was doing a pretty thorough job of fucking him hard and fast and completely. He could see one way out that was more surefire than any other—walk away. Leave the country. Forget Jabberwock and Reagan and everything else attached to his life.

But he was starting to get an idea of why Reagan was so driven. Jabberwock's people were destroying their lives. Obliterating Blake's freedom, because Jabberwock liked games.

If Blake stayed to pursue this, though, he put Reagan at risk. She wasn't a wanted felon.

A key rattled in the lock, knocking his thoughts offline. He reached for his gun and leveled it at the door. He thumbed off the safety and looked down the sights.

"It's me." Reagan's voice carried through the insulated plywood.

He breathed out as he lowered his weapon, and she stepped into the room.

She eyed his hands. "I'll try to remember to announce myself sooner next time."

"I appreciate that." He holstered the sidearm. "How'd it go?"

She held up the keys. "Ready for a road trip?"

"Toss me the keys." He held out his hand.

She frowned and tucked them into her pocket. "No. You need to be the passenger, so you can stay better hidden from the cameras."

"You and I aren't staying together. We're going our separate ways," he said. That was the main flaw he saw with pursuing Jabberwock. Blake didn't think he could keep Reagan safe.

"Bullshit. Do you remember less than a week ago, when I tried to tell you the same thing? Nope. Nuh-uh. You're stuck with me, or you can get your own ride."

"Fine. I'll locate my own transportation." He brushed past her.

She grabbed his arm and spun him back to face her. "Don't—" Her voice cracked, and she hissed. "Don't walk out like that." She spoke in a more even tone. "If I were Queen, would you pulling this *I can't protect you, so I can't stay with you* bullshit?"

"I wouldn't have trusted her in the first place. She had my back, but only as far as it benefited her.

This isn't just about keeping you safe. You don't have an APB on you, so you can go wherever you want, without fear of being caught. If you stay with me, you lose that freedom"

She studied him for a moment. "Do you trust me?"

"You're the one who was struggling with trust." He should have said *yes*. Why didn't he?

"It's true you're the one with your face plastered on every news channel and feed." She leaned against the door, blocking it. "The way I see it, if you were trying to fuck me over at this point, you'd leave. Or report me as your associate, but that would make you as mad as the man hunting us. So yes, I trust you. For now." She winked. The expression didn't mask the seriousness that lay under her teasing.

"Me too," he said.

"Good. Let's go."

He was grateful she didn't ask him to clarify what he meant by *me too*. He wasn't sure he could. As they headed into the parking lot, he realized they were walking toward a Subaru that had to be at least thirty years old. "How do we know that thing won't fall apart on us?"

"We don't." She slid into the driver's side. "But it only has to get us out of town and to a place where we can buy another one."

He hoped she had more of that optimism. Something told him it kept her going, and now would be an unfortunate time for it to give out. He dropped into the passenger seat, keeping his hood low over his face. It gnawed at him that he couldn't do this as well on his own. With her anonymity, she could go places he couldn't. But if she was willing to put her faith in him, he could return the favor.

They drove for about an hour before they crossed into Kentucky. The more distance they put between them and the raid on the hotel, the easier Blake could breathe. Because of the time of year, the sun would set in an hour or two, making it easier to hide their faces from traffic cameras, and then he'd take his turn driving. At least then he'd feel like he was contributing.

"Since we're moving into trusting-each-other territory, can I ask you something?" Blake said. "And don't tell me *you just did.*"

She smirked. "Take the fun out of it. Sure. Fire away. But know I may not answer."

"You said Alex's code led you to a few things already. What kind of things?"

"Nothing that's significant on its own. For instance, there's a deed to the house I was born in— apparently he purchased it before he died."

As opposed to after? Blake bit back the sarcastic retort. It might be funny in his head, but it wouldn't help the mood. "He was nostalgic, then?"

"He wasn't. Not the Alex I remember. He was practical and ordered." She sighed. "But it becomes clearer to me every day, I didn't know the real Alex."

The perfect segue for Blake's next question. "You mentioned a journal. That sounds fairly sentimental to me."

"Not necessarily, but in his case, it was." Traffic slowed as they merged with evening commuters. Reagan looked at ease behind the wheel, despite the sadness on her face. This must have been a lot of her days after he and she split.

"I shouldn't pry. I'm sorry." Curiosity boiled inside, but if the journal was private, it wasn't information he needed.

"It's okay." This was a melancholy sight. He'd seen a lot of sides to Reagan, but the raw sadness without anger behind it was new. "It'd be nice to talk to someone about it, rather than locking it all in my head. Sometimes it gets crowded up there."

"I know the feeling. And I'm listening."

"It's been hard to get through. Partly for emotional reasons—there's some personal stuff in there—but mostly because he had shitty handwriting. It's like deciphering another language. He mentions a woman—someone he loved. I'm going through each page with a fine-toothed comb, looking for any clue I can find."

"Is where you went this morning related to that?" he asked.

She clenched the steering wheel and her jaw. "That didn't have anything to do with the journal."

The abrupt shift in mood caught him off guard. He wanted to push but didn't want her to shut him out. Maybe a different angle. "I hope you weren't up long. I don't want to slow you down."

"You didn't, but I don't sleep much." Her tone shifted to cool and clinical.

Which reminded him of another question she probably wouldn't answer. "Is that related at all to the pills you took?"

"What pills?"

Digging into her personal life wasn't his right, but if she'd gotten herself addicted to something that had withdrawal or other symptoms, he needed to know. "The unmarked bottle, last night."

"Nothing illegal. Not prescription or opioid."

"That's oddly specific." The evasion didn't reassure him.

A low growl echoed from her throat. "It's a combination of caffeine, ginseng, and B vitamins. Standard over-the-counter energy supplement."

In a warehouse-store-sized bottle. "How often are you taking it?"

"Only when I have the dreams."

"You have to sleep sometimes." He couldn't put the force that he should behind the words. He'd done the same thing when he got back from deployment.

"I sleep. I stay awake until I collapse from exhaustion, then rinse and repeat."

That's not healthy, died in his throat. Who was he, to lecture her on best ways to deal with the past? He had experience, but that didn't mean he'd done it right.

"Anyway. Alex." Her cool removed tone was back. "The clue we're following now was one of the toughest to crack. Even after I figured it out, I had to find the key to the safety deposit box. I have it, though. Rather, I think I do. I hope."

"Me too." He couldn't think of anything better to say.

Silence descended over the car. When they

cleared the slog of traffic, she found a good cruising speed again.

Red and blue lights reflected off the glass and the interior of the car, and the sound of a siren ratcheted Blake's pulse. They were being pulled over.

Reagan changed lanes until she could park on the shoulder.

"What the fuck are you doing?" He couldn't keep the growl from his voice. His fake law enforcement ID would only make things worse if the cop recognized him as the guy plastered on APB's.

"We're not going to run." Despite her casual tone, her knuckles were white on the steering wheel. "Follow my lead. We'll be fine."

He didn't like going into this blind. He watched in the side mirror as the officer approached the car. Reagan sniffled and rubbed her eyes.

The cop knocked on her glass, and she rolled down the window with a sob.

Really? Blake's internal sarcasm meter climbed along with his apprehension. She was trying to cry her way out of a ticket?

"Evening, miss." The officer shone his light into the car, over Blake, and back to Reagan. "Do you know why I pulled you over?"

"I don't know." She spoke with a soft southern accent, and her voice cracked on the last word. "Was I speeding? Oh God. I'm so sorry. I should have been paying closer attention. I'm just… Was I speeding?"

"Your tags are out of date."

She choked back a sob. "I'm sorry. I'm

borrowing it from my friend. I don't have a car of my own, and our mother passed away this morning, and we need to get to Maine, and—damn it—I'm sorry. You don't want to hear about any of this. It's just the whole thing was so sudden, and we didn't know, and I don't know what I'm going to do."

"I understand, miss." The cop's voice softened. He shone the light toward Blake again. "Sir, are you her husband or boyfriend? Maybe you should be driving."

"He's my brother." Reagan spoke before Blake could. "He and Momma were so close, he can't see straight. I shouldn't tell you that. God, he'd kill me if he could think. Don't have me towed, please? We need to get to Momma."

"I understand." The officer put his flashlight away.

Blake bit back his shock. The man didn't even ask for license and registration. *Fuck me.*

"I'm going to let you off with a warning this time." The officer stepped back. "As soon as you get back home, have your friend register their car."

"Of course. Thank you, sir. Momma would have liked you."

"I'm sure she would have. Drive safely." The man patted the roof of the car.

Reagan pulled back onto the road as soon as the officer was back in his vehicle. She checked her mirror every few seconds.

Blake didn't know whether to be impressed or terrified. "Pull into a nearby neighborhood."

She nodded and took the next exit. Blake had her navigate subdivision streets until they found one that was mostly dark. "Stay here. Keep an eye out." He squeezed her hand.

He hated doing this, but it would keep them from being pulled over again until they could find another vehicle. He pulled the registration sticker from a Tennessee license plate and stuck it on the battered Subaru, then tucked a couple hundred dollars under their windshield wiper. With any luck, the owner would be the one to find the cash, and it would make up for them having to wait in line at the DMV for new stickers.

Less than two minutes later, he was back in the car, and they were on the freeway again, heading north.

"You scare me sometimes," he said.

"Because I know how to cry, to get out of a ticket? You shot two men without hesitation last night, but *I* scare *you*."

"Well…" He shrugged in the darkness.

She scrubbed her eyes. "I don't have mad sniper skills. I had to survive somehow."

The more time he spent with her, the better a grasp he got on how she'd done exactly that. It was smart. When he thought about it, he'd be disappointed to hear otherwise.

Chapter Sixteen

Sawyer wasn't supposed to know Kurt Donovan was the proxy for one of the State's senators, but Jabberwock knew everything about the people he dealt with. From the moment he scheduled the first *cleaning* appointment for Kurt, he'd had all the vital information for the man and everyone Kurt worked for or with.

"We— I'm looking at moving into a new market." Kurt's gaze flitted from the trees to the sidewalk, to the two men walking behind them, then forward again. He was almost as bad at looking inconspicuous as those same two men in suits, strolling through the park in the middle of November—the bodyguards who looked like they should be watching a senator, not a squirrelly guy in slacks and Patagonia fleece.

Lisa was a solo power-walker, sometimes pushing ahead of them and other times falling back. That woman excelled at blending in. Or she would, if anyone besides the group was around to see her.

Sawyer wrapped his jacket tighter against the wind. Thankfully, it wasn't too bitter this far south.

"Define this *market*."

"It's… uh… I have clients looking to pay pennies on the dollar for access to untraceable funds. This is untapped stuff."

Sawyer doubted that last bit, but he got paid either way. Hell—if things didn't pan out, he might be connecting the money supplier and the cleaner next. He spun the rest of the words through his head, looking for whatever hidden meaning they were supposed to hold. In the past, he'd hooked Kurt—or rather, Kurt's employer—up with someone who *eliminated any stain or pest, no matter how big or small.* That was a straightforward concept. *Untraceable funds* could hold a wide number of definitions. If they were talking resale, that narrowed things down. He guessed the guy wanted to buy credit-card numbers.

"I have a contact who can provide funds only traced back to the original owner. Will that work?" Sawyer said. It was stupid to be vague. Anyone listening would know the conversation wasn't on the up-and-up. But talking this way wasn't an admission of guilt; it simply sounded suspicious to the outside observer. That was good enough for Sawyer.

"That's perfect." Kurt looked behind him again, then clenched his fists.

Sawyer didn't like the change in posture, and he casually drifted his hand toward the holster hidden on his hip. Kurt probably wouldn't notice. The bodyguards would. Lisa definitely would. "But? I hear a *but* in there." He kept his tone as cool as the weather.

"What happened at the masquerade in

Nashville… People are saying, if Jabberwock's presence draws federal and media attention—"

"That didn't have anything to do with me."

A dog barked somewhere outside the park. The closest indicator they'd had of company all afternoon.

"I'm not the one saying it"—Kurt held up his hands—"but you have to admit… An armed robbery, where you happen to be, on the same night Hatter emerges from the dead? A guy who's apparently an ex-fed? The appeal of your service is anonymity. If you can't provide that…"

Fury sliced through Sawyer's veins, white-hot and chasing away the kiss of fall on his face. He grabbed Kurt by the collar, pushed him back into a tree, and planted his arm against Kurt's windpipe, while he pressed the barrel of his pistol to Kurt's temple. "Does anyone know who you really are or what you're up to?" Sawyer let the growl roll through his question.

"*Stand down*," one of the bodyguards said, and the twin sound of hammers being cocked greeted Sawyer.

He didn't have to look or hear a noise from Lisa, to know she'd drawn her gun. She wouldn't waste precious seconds with an unneeded gesture, to simply make her actions known.

"It's all right, guys." Kurt's voice shook. "We're all pals here." He looked at Sawyer. "They're holstering their side arms. We're just talking, you and me. Right?"

"Sure. Talk away." Sawyer pressed the steel harder against Kurt's skull.

"You've kept us quiet up till now. It's true. But how long until a slipup like the other night changes things?"

Sawyer clenched his jaw, and rage spilled inside at having his ability questioned. "*Things* change a lot faster if some chicken-shit senator's lackey gets cold feet because of an unfortunate coincidence. The system works because everyone does their part. I've done mine."

"But can you continue to?"

"You've got balls." Sawyer chuckled and stepped back. He was still furious, but had to respect the other man. "Not many people can keep up their half an argument with a gun pressed to their head."

Kurt's laugh was stuttered. He smoothed out his jacket and kept several feet between him and Sawyer. "I'm glad we can work this out."

"Me too." Sawyer leveled his weapon and pulled the trigger, hitting the tree next to Kurt's head and sending splinters flying. "It'd be a shame if someone spilled your secrets."

"Are you threatening me?" Kurt's indignation was weak, compared to the way his hands shook.

"I like the word *extortion*. In more ways than one." Sawyer waved his gun. "You know, on second thought, I don't think I can hook you up with a new contact. Thank you for reaching out, though."

He turned and strolled toward the parking lot, and Lisa fell into step beside him. Kurt's shouted protests grew more distant until Sawyer and Lisa cut them off by sliding into the back of their waiting car.

The driver started the engine and navigated

them into traffic.

"I don't think the whole mentally-unstable, Joker, I-just-want-to-watch-the-world-burn thing is a good look for you," Lisa said.

Sawyer's anger surged back, cooler this time, and he suppressed it. He needed to have an actual conversation with her, not something that deteriorated. "Do you think it was a mistake to tell people who I really am? To show Jabberwock's face?"

She slid lower in her seat, to rest her head against the back. "You want a *yes* or *no* answer, and the issue isn't that cut and dried."

"Don't make me decipher vague responses and riddles. I'm not in the mood." He stared out the tinted windows at the passing scenery. They could be on the fringes of any medium-sized city. Freeways surrounded a few buildings in the middle of it all tried to reach the sky but didn't quite. He forced himself to sink into the familiar sights and dial back his mood.

"It's the proverbial rock and a hard place."

He rolled his eyes and looked at her. "Idioms aren't helping either."

"You had to do something, after Hatter. Showing yourself is having its drawbacks, but staying in the shadows would have too. It's too late to second-guess the decision and put Jabberwock back in the bottle."

"It wasn't this hard after White Rabbit."

Lisa pursed her lips and furrowed her brow.

"It's true." Another lie he told Alice, in the sea of hundreds. Alex didn't embezzle; he betrayed

Lisa. Sawyer told Alice otherwise because he was curious to see if she knew more than she was letting on. Did she have more information about Alex than Sawyer did? It didn't seem that way.

Lisa fiddled with the end of her ponytail. "Alex made a mistake that we kept between us. Blake worked for the NSA. The two situations are hardly comparable."

She had a point. "All right. I'll dial back the show of crazy." He could make a few concessions. "But we need to get a grip on things."

"You're telling me."

Chapter Seventeen

Blake pressed the button on the water fountain more out of habit than because he expected it to be turned on. There was no shock when water didn't come out. He was far more surprised the rest-stop bathrooms were unlocked and the toilets working.

While he waited for Reagan, he wandered to the picnic table at the edge of the property. Splinters of paint bit through his jeans when he sat on the bench. He pulled out the phone they used for navigation. Between the two of them, they'd set up the Wi-Fi on the device to constantly be searching for new hotspots. It would piggyback on one, ride it to the next signal, and hop several more times before connecting to the internet.

The device should be untraceable as theirs, but if someone did manage to figure out who owned it, they'd have a hell of a time finding out where it was, before Reagan and Blake moved on.

The bitter air chapping his face had him concerned. They'd picked up winter coats and warmer clothes when they hit southern Indiana, but the bite in the wind held a threat he knew from childhood. He slid up the weather for the region. The line-drawing cloud with flakes falling from it made him scowl. It wasn't enough information.

The *-7 F* next to the icon was more telling. He clicked through, for details.

"What's up?" Reagan's question jarred him, and his hand flew to his holster out of instinct.

He should be keeping a better eye on his surroundings, but this was bad. "There's a blizzard blowing through. We need to find a place for the night, and soon."

"No." She slid in next to him, her arm pressing against his, and took the phone. "We're so close. We push through."

He was fine with her being confident and headstrong, but this was something he wouldn't budge on. "Have you ever driven in a Midwestern blizzard?"

"I've driven in a Utah one."

"Would you do it willingly?"

She stood, and he fell into step beside her, as they returned to the car. "I'm not doing most of this *willingly*. It's more of a need than a want," she said.

"Fair point." He wouldn't ask if that included his company. "This has the potential to make what you've seen look like a couple of flakes. Six feet overnight isn't the kind of thing you fuck with."

She stopped at the passenger side and rested her arms on the top of the car to look at him. "I hate how long it's taking to get there."

"If that safety deposit box has sat untouched for five years, it will still be there if we take an extra day or two to get to it."

"It's snow."

He swallowed a snarl. "And you know how to drive in it. Good for you. It's not just the snow that's the problem; it's when it stops. If we get stuck in it, and the clouds clear out and the wind kicks up, negative seven will sound like paradise." He wished he were exaggerating.

She sighed in frustration and tossed him the keys. "You win."

He'd pick another time to be smug. The clouds overhead didn't look forgiving, and the closest town was fifty miles out.

Wind howled outside their hotel room. Blake sat on the bed, back to the wall and legs stretch out in front of him. Reagan lay on her back, head on his thigh, alternating her gaze between the ceiling and him.

"You seemed pretty emphatic about the weather." Her tone was pleasant and soft. "Firsthand knowledge?"

Instinct and years of experience glossing over the details of his past wanted him to say, *I've heard and didn't see any reason to risk it.* He didn't have to do that with her, though. Though he didn't completely trust her motives, there was a lot he was okay with her knowing. More than most people ever learned about him. The realization struck him. "I grew up in Elmhurst. It's a suburb of Chicago."

A tiny smile played on her face, and she twisted her head in his direction. "Will we drive through there on our way?"

"Probably not. It's not directly off the freeway."

"Do you miss it?"

"Do you miss home?"

"Sometimes." A frown flickered in before vanishing. "But it never felt like home after Alex was gone. It's as if… Never mind."

Ice pelted the windows, and the lights dimmed before staying on bright and strong.

Blake brushed a strand of hair off Reagan's forehead. "As if what?"

"You'll think it's stupid or that I'm broken, or something."

"I doubt that."

She pushed into a sitting position, crossed her legs, and looked at him. "Sometimes I feel, until six months ago, I was wandering lost, not really belonging anywhere. I'm not saying I love the life I live now, but at least I'm the guiding force, rather than being tossed about by the wind."

"I get that." He gave her a sad smile. "And no, I don't miss home. I miss the memory of what it was when I was younger, but that place doesn't exist. Maybe it never did, the way childhood-me sees it."

Wind whistled through cracks in the door, shrill and icy. Fortunately, the extra blankets the hotel gave them sat tucked at the foot of the bed, waiting for use.

"Did you really want to be Spiderman when you grew up?" she asked.

He'd forgotten he told her that. Those first days in the diner, when he was still a double agent, seemed like a lifetime ago. "I did. Though it turns out

I'm allergic to spiders, so I might not have survived that first step toward great power."

"I never liked Spiderman. No offense."

"None taken. I'm not him. You more of a Wonder Woman girl?"

She rolled her eyes, but it didn't mar her smile. "I tended toward Spawn. Azrael. Constantine. The Crow."

"Avenging angels?"

"And damned souls. They always felt more real to me." Her laugh was tinged with something dark. "As real as a guy returning from the dead to wreak havoc on those who wronged him can be."

"We're actively trying to destroy a man who named himself after a fictional character from a children's book. I don't see why they can't be real."

She crawled forward on the mattress, to sit next to him. When she leaned her head against his shoulder, he wrapped an arm around her. He wasn't sure why this always felt natural, but she never pulled away, and he never second-guessed it.

Silence descended over the room, interrupted by the occasional shrill of the storm trying to get at them.

"Is that why you enlisted in the Marines?" she asked. "Closest you could get to being Spiderman?"

"More or less. I'm not drawing the same parallel for you. Code-breaking and hacking don't fall in line with avenging angels."

"Really?" She glanced up at him from under her eyelashes. "After everything I've seen and said and done, you don't think vengeance is involved?"

He did. It was the biggest concern he had, and

what kept him from placing more faith in her. The knowledge knocked his thoughts off kilter. "Do you want my super hero response?"

"No. But go ahead."

"If getting back at Jabberwock is the only thing keeping you going, what do you do when he's gone?"

"How did you go from Marine to NSA?" she asked.

He bit the inside of his cheek at the way she dodged his question without hesitation. He wouldn't push, because that would make her close off further. "The scars on my shoulder? I caught stray friendly fire when I was in Afghanistan. It sent me home, earned me a discharge, and cost me my direction."

Saying the words clenched around his heart in a way he didn't expect. It had been years since he talked about this. It shouldn't still bother him. He forced down the reaction. "I was lost and spending a lot of time online, and I discovered the deep web. I'd seen evil before. Hell—I fought it face to face.

But then I saw things for sale. Drugs, money, guns, people…" He shook his head, but it didn't clear out the creeping darkness. "I started figuring out how to track it. Digging. Pretending to be someone I wasn't. Learning to trace IP addresses. Setting them up to be arrested. I sucked at hiding myself, though."

"You?" Teasing lined her question.

"Give me a sniper rifle and a good spotter, and no one will see me. The NSA watched my activity. I inadvertently made it easier for them because I did a lot of it from VA computers. They approached me. Told me they had resources if I was willing to learn. I was."

"Your cause sounds a lot nobler than mine." She snuggled closer and pulled his arm tighter around her.

It had been. Until he figured out the bad guys walked both sides of the line. Until he saw what some of his colleagues were willing to do for results—the lines they crossed and the collateral damage they caused. "I guess that's one way to look at it."

Chapter Eighteen

"Do you know why I slept with you in Las Vegas?" Reagan's question caught Blake off guard.

"I'm a smooth-talking bastard?"

She laughed and ducked her head. "That didn't hurt. Nor did that you're attractive, intelligent, s—" She cringed.

"Don't let me stop you from listing my amazing qualities," he said playfully. He wanted the cloud that had moved into the room to clear out and take the less pleasant aspects of the past with it.

"Safe. I was going to say *safe*, which contradicts the rest of the story, and now you've ruined it." Her pout was exaggerated and teasing, but a shadow lay under her gaze.

He didn't know how to deal with the confession. It sank deep, soothing and incinerating at the same time. "I didn't mean to interrupt the narrative. Forget I asked for clarification."

She frowned, but it vanished under a blank mask. "Anyway. All that other stuff aside, you approached me right after Wayne…" A pained look crossed her face, and she drew in a shaky breath.

"After the last time he freaked out because he thought we were in danger, and I didn't believe him. You and I were in a public place. There was the rush of getting caught. The thrill of doing this naughty thing. The fact that you were a stranger. It was so much about the adrenaline."

On some level, he'd expected her confession to sound deep and heartfelt, but not be sincere. His brain wasn't prepared for something like, *I did it for the high*. Then again, it was a motive he understood. He didn't like all this waiting-to-see-if-it-was-safe-to-take-the-next-step stuff. He'd rather look whatever they were dealing with in the eye, through a high-powered scope, and see if this was the one time he didn't get the shot off first. "I'm glad I could be there for you."

"Did you really think I knew who you were?" she asked.

He wanted to be offended that she still questioned his word on that, but then he'd have to admit how much of what she said he still didn't take at face value. "Yes. Wayne swore on a number of occasions that he'd told you he was working with someone on the inside, and who I was."

"I wonder why he never said anything."

"He was Wayne. He lived and died by his paranoia." Blake cringed. "Sorry. Poor choice of words."

"Appropriate."

"Why did you do it, in Salt Lake?" he asked. It might not be something he wanted to hear, but if they were going to traipse through their sex life, might as well go in deep.

She pulled from his grasp and knelt, studying him. "I think… I think I needed to know something was real." She poked him in the shoulder, where his scars sat under his shirt. "There's this nagging doubt that's been there since I started digging into Jabberwock, five years ago, that maybe none of it is real. Even now."

"Funny. You feel like you're trapped in a nightmare, and every morning, when I wake up, I hope the better part of the last decade was just a dream. All of it, except…"

She tilted her head to the side, curiosity breaking through the melancholy. "Except what?"

"You." It was an odd thing to admit. As strange as hearing that she saw him as being safe. But he was unwilling to take it back.

The pink that spread across her cheeks was alluring. "Shameless flatterer."

"I've been called worse." He settled a hand on her face and leaned in to brush his lips over hers. White-hot sparks sped through him, banishing the chill, and he deepened the kiss.

Her groan and the tingle of her mouth against his, were like a finely aged brandy—smooth, intense, and carrying a hard burn through him. He knotted his fingers in her hair and held her captive, needing to vanish into the moment.

Her mewl drove to his core, sucking him further into now. "Don't start this if you're not prepared to finish it." There was a pleading in her voice. A quiet desperation that made him think she was talking about more than the sex.

He broke away to clear his thoughts, but

looking at the smattering of freckles on her nose that were only noticeable up close, the flush on her lips, and the chaos in her eyes that matched his own, did the opposite.

He brushed his lips up the side of her neck, and she tilted her head back, exposing more skin. If he let go, would this all evaporate? No. He refused to let that happen.

He pushed her sweater up, to settle his palm on her waist. Sharp bursts of desire and memory flowed between them. He shoved her top and bra out of the way, then kissed a path down to her breast.

She arched her back when he reached her nipple. He flicked his tongue over the hard nub, and her squeal of delight traveled over him to tug at his cock. With a quick push and twist, he rolled her onto her back and knelt above her, straddling her.

The wicked smile she treated him to danced over his senses. When he lowered his head to her breast again and scrapped his teeth across her nipple, she twisted under him, hips coming off the ground, her pelvis colliding with his.

He dropped his hand to her stomach, and then slid lower. He didn't pause when he reached jeans, popping the button open and yanking the fabric apart to split the zipper.

She sighed when he dipped below her panties and glided over her lower lips. Her soft sounds and the way she yielded beneath him, when she so often refused to budge in daily life, thrummed in his veins.

"Fuck. You're amazing." He spoke against her skin, not wanting to pull away from the intoxication of tasting her.

When he slid his hand between her wet folds, she bucked her hips and moaned. She ground against his fingers when he placed one on either side of her clit and stroked. "Harder."

He wasn't sure what she wanted more of, but he was willing to give her everything. He nibbled and massaged her aching center.

Her rhythmic writhing taunted him with memories of what it was like to be buried inside her. His erection strained against his pants, aching and almost raw.

He increased his pace, and she bucked against his hand. The incredible noises she made grew to staccato cries, pulsing against his shaft. He adored the way her face scrunched up, her lips slightly parted and her eyes closed, when she was near orgasm.

Blake pushed harder, and she lifted her ass off the mattress when she came, pressing into his touch until she dropped away with a shuddering sigh.

Her screams shredded his control. He moved his mouth back to hers, lightly stroking her but not touching the swollen nub between her legs. The way she returned the kiss begged for her to be devoured. He tangled his fingers in her hair and held her captive, while he glided his lips to her ear, to nip at her lobe.

"Fuck me, please?" Her soft question washed over him with lust.

He nodded, not sure he could manage more than a grunt in response, as he yanked off his sweatshirt. He unsnapped her bra and dragged it down her arms.

His desire surged when he took in her bare nipples, red and swollen from the attention he'd given them.

She wriggled out of her jeans and panties, each new twist of her hips scraping friction across his thighs.

He stood to strip off the rest of his clothes, his cock springing free the moment it found a way out of his boxers. He trailed his gaze over figure on the bed, drinking in every inch and curve and delicious glint of temptation.

Condom. Right.

Tearing it from the foil and rolling it on wasted precious seconds Blake didn't want to surrender.

He straddled her again, and she reached between his legs to grip his shaft and move her hand in a steady stroke. He half-closed his eyes, moaning at her tender touch. "So good. So amazing."

She guided him toward her slick tunnel, teasing him by brushing the head of his cock along her slit. When she dipped near her opening, he couldn't hold back. He thrust forward.

She withdrew her hand, leaving him free to plunge deep inside her.

He fell into the sensation of her wrapped around him—her legs around his waist, her arms over his shoulders, and her pussy gripping his shaft.

They rocked against each other. He tried to set a slow pace, but she pushed back, and he didn't have the willpower to resist. A sharp bolt of arousal sparked through him at the heat between them, and he pounded harder and faster.

He used one hand beside her head to hold himself up, and used the other to massage her breast, pinching her nipple and rolling it between his fingers.

The assault on his senses, from her moans to her warmth, to the joy lingering on her lips, tore through him, and he couldn't hold back. His balls tightened, begging for release. He tried to draw the moment out, wanting to stay here forever, but he didn't have that kind of willpower. Climax rushed over him.

His grunts—or maybe it was the fact he pounded harder—seemed to nudge her over the edge again. She dug her nails into his back and gasped as she came, clenching around his spasming cock and drawing his orgasm toward *uncomfortable*, but leaving him on this side of *incredible*.

He slammed insider her, until he couldn't any more, then slowed to a stop. When he opened his eyes, she was looking up at him, a sweet smile teasing her lips. The deceptive innocence, mischief lurking beneath, was almost enough to make him hard again.

He stripped off and disposed of the condom, then dropped onto the bed and pulled her to him.

Blake sank into the warmth and weight of Reagan lying next to him, the way he did so many nights. He always told himself it was a matter of comfort—two people with the same goal, who needed someone to lean on.

He didn't believe that lie anymore. This was about her. Keeping her safe. Falling for her—God help him, he was. And when it all crumbled, it was going to hurt like hell. Knowing that didn't give him the power to change what he felt.

Chapter Nineteen

Waking up to Reagan gone was becoming as familiar to Blake as falling asleep next to her. It took him a couple of years and some serious narcotics to get past his insomnia and nightmares. She didn't take that route, so he wouldn't complain.

He showered and dressed, and she still hadn't returned. Might as well step outside and see how badly they were snowed in.

When he opened the motel room door, the early sun glared off snow and made him wince. He stepped back to grab his sunglasses. Despite the blinding light, the chill bit into his cheeks.

Snow was pushed toward the edges of the parking lot, reaching more than a foot over his head. It looked like the storm wasn't as bad as he feared, but with the clouds gone, it would have gotten icy overnight, so roads would still be treacherous.

A flash of color in the midst of grays caught his attention, and he turned to see Reagan standing several feet from the back of the building. She was gazing out over an empty field.

He approached, not trying to mask the crunch

of his boots, but she didn't turn.

"What are you looking at?" he asked when he reached her.

She nodded at the Chicago skyline. Buildings raced toward the sky, jutting from the horizon. "It's so flat."

"Are you missing the mountains?"

She shook her head. "Just making an observation."

"How long have you been up?"

She finally looked at him. "A few hours. Someday you'll have to teach me how to sleep the way you do."

"Someday I hope I can." It was an odd thing to wish for, but with their situation as topsy-turvy as it was, it seemed as good as anything.

She nodded toward the car. "Do you feel better about getting back on the road this morning?"

"Yes. The roads should still be mostly empty. We'll have to drive slowly, but the sky is clear and so is the forecast. We should be fine."

She handed him the keys. "You drive. I want to read you something from Alex's journal and get your opinion on it."

"Sure." Now he was curious.

Half an hour later, they'd checked out and were on their way to Minnesota again. Blake was right about the traffic—very few people were braving the ice- and snow-packed freeway. The driving was slow but doable, and better than waiting in a room.

Reagan hadn't said much beyond basic *yeses* and *nos*.

Blake tried to be patient, to let her bring up the journal topic again, but a little nudge wouldn't hurt. "What did you want to read me?"

"Oh right." She leaned forward in her seat, to grab something from the bag between her legs, then sat up again. "I found a passage this morning. Most of what's in here is Alex talking to the book or leaving notes to himself. Musings. But this one… *Kitten, I don't know if you ever found this, but if you did, I pray to God you're all right.*"

"Are you *kitten*?" The passage was easy to make sense of, in a basic way. But what was hidden behind it?

"I'm not done," she said. "It continues. *If Reagan is with you, give her my love.*"

A chill that wasn't a result of the weather ran down Blake's spine. "So who's *kitten*?"

"Apparently she's this mysterious love of his life. He mentions her a lot, but this is the first time I've found a passage where he speaks to her directly. Another bit of him I didn't know about."

"That's kind of sweet." He was both touched and bothered by the idea of love letters from beyond the grave.

"Hmm…" She chuckled.

"What?"

"I hadn't shared the parts about her with you, because I didn't think you'd care for the sappiness."

"Are you saying I'm not romantic?"

"Your words, not mine. I didn't say anything of the sort. Though…" She put the journal away. "What was it you told me that first day? *How do you feel about leaving these stuffy suits behind and letting me fuck you until you can't walk?"*

"That's not fair. You admitted you fucked me that day for the adrenaline rush. What other kinds of things did Alex write about this mystery woman?"

"That he never met anyone like her. That he couldn't believe she noticed him. That every time he looked at her, all he saw was the future." Her voice cracked. "Sorry."

"It's okay. I didn't mean to drag up painful memories. It sounds like he really loved her."

"Yeah, it does." There was a wistfulness in Reagan's voice. "Must have been nice."

The same thing she said in Nashville, about having someone he trusted. Would she and he ever reach the point where they could have that? Trust? Adoration?

The car hit an icy patch, and his gut lurched. Instinct kicked in, and he steered with the skid, struggling to right the vehicle without overcorrecting. He didn't have any control, though. None of the tires gripped.

The drift from the road down the side of the shoulder seemed to move in slow motion, dragging his heart into his shoes as they slid and stopped with the passenger door against a tree.

For a second, he didn't dare breathe, then he let out a long gasp and looked at Reagan. "Are you all right?"

"Yes." She was pale but looked intact.

She'd never screamed. Or made a sound. She kept her cool the entire time. The realization felt oddly clinical.

He unbuckled his seatbelt, climbed from the

car, and helped Reagan do the same.

"What now?" she asked.

He tried to check for a nearby tow-truck. His fingers were icy in under a minute, jabbing painfully at the screen of the phone. He snarled and jammed the device back into his pocket. "We're so far in the middle of nowhere, there are no tow-truck numbers coming up in a search."

"That sucks. So we walk to the nearest service station, to get someone to tow us back up to the road, and hope we get picked up before then?"

Sounded like a plan.

They should have bought sturdier boots. Heavier jackets. Snow spilled over the tops of his shoes. Their feet would be numb at best, by the time they made it to the next exit.

They trudged back to the freeway, where the snow was packed down the most. The subzero temperatures made conversation a bad idea. They tucked their heads down, kept close to each other— so they knew they were both still here—and walked.

His face and legs and ears and everything were frozen by the time they reached an exit, and by his calculations, it had only been half an hour. The warmth of the gas station called to him, and they approached.

The flash of the TV caught his eye, his own picture staring back at him. "Fuck." He stalled a few feet back from the entrance.

She looked between him and the news. "I'll be back." Concern and sympathy hung in her voice. "Find someplace warm?"

"I will."

She kissed him on the cheek. The warmth of her lips branded itself on his skin. "I'll hurry. And I promise to drive safely."

He didn't doubt any of it, but he still hated to let her go alone. He fucking hated every bit of this. Being wanted. How useless it made him. Watching her walk away and having to wait and hope she came back.

And he hated most of all that he still had that doubt—that nagging feeling that, one of these days, she wouldn't return.

Chapter Twenty

Sawyer was grateful to be back in the war room. The rest of his meetings had gone smoothly, including one establishing contact with a new vendor. It was a nice contrast to the weeks of chaos, but it still felt good to be home.

The quiet tap of keys filled the room, replacing any need for conversation while he and Lisa worked.

A familiar chime sounded from his phone—the tone indicating Jabberwock had a secured message from one of his people. Sawyer pulled up the note and frowned at the name in his inbox. *Hatter*.

Whispers flitted through his veins, tightening in his neck. That account was shut within hours of discovering Blake was a double agent. What was it doing, active?

I'm in Lakeville, MN. Or rather, your ex-Hatter is.

Cheshire Cat.

"What the fuck?" Sawyer stared at the message, tension winding toward a headache. He hadn't been able to locate Alice and Blake since they left Nashville, and now this arrogant jackass Cat was sending him Blake's location from a dead email address?

"What's wrong?" Lisa asked.

He showed her the phone. "Do you think this is funny?"

She crossed the room, squinted at the words, and scowled. "Not even close."

"Then you didn't send it?"

"Why would I do that? You're the one with the fucked-up sense of humor."

He turned the device back toward him and stared at the note for several seconds. "Do you think it's true?"

"That Blake is in Minnesota? Hell if I know." Lisa settled back into her beanbag but didn't grab her laptop.

Sawyer needed to know how the message got to him, but he also couldn't leave the lead untapped. It wasn't as though he'd chase it himself, though. "We have a vendor with suppliers out there, don't we? Put out feelers, see if anyone's heard anything and if Blake and Alice are still together."

"Sure. I'm not doing anything else."

He frowned at the sarcasm. "Unless I'm inconveniencing you."

"No. This is fine," she said through clenched teeth.

He'd dig into her issue later, off the clock. "Good. If it's him, find out what he's doing there. He doesn't have any holdings, and neither of them has ties to the past." Jabberwock liked a good game of

Cat and mouse, but not when he was the mouse. What was Cat trying to accomplish by sending him this?

"Maybe they're chasing ghosts." She shrugged. "Since you've re-tasked me, I have the other information you wanted."

He'd almost forgotten. She was finding names for him—the people assigned to Blake's manhunt. "Is it good?"

The corner of her mouth tugged up, and the joy in her eyes was cruel. "It's better than good. Lead on the case is Blake's old boss. He was in charge of operations in Seattle when they grabbed Reagan— the guy who got approval to give her a long leash, at Blake's prompting. And he made the decision to leave Blake in contact with her, despite knowing their… explicit past."

"Send me his info." Sawyer understood her expression now. Glee tempered his irritation at the out-of-the-blue email that shouldn't be. And see if you can figure out where Blake and Alice are going next."

Lisa raised her brows. "Because I'm psychic? I don't know why they're in Minnesota, or if they are even there. How am I supposed to tell you what their next stop is?"

That was twice in rapid succession. She was probably stressed. The last few weeks had been rough. He'd make things up to her when this mess was straightened out. "If you could, I'd appreciate it." He softened his tone. "I know you'll find me everything that's out there, even if no one else could."

"Fine. Then they're heading to Tampa next." She bit off the words.

That was where one of his larger offices was set up. One no one should be able to connect him to. "That's not any funnier than the message from Cat."

"None of this is funny." She grabbed her phone and stood. "Good luck with your NSA guy. I'm going to make some calls up north."

She strolled from the room, jabbing her screen.

Tampa Bay. She just tossed that out there, didn't she? Something was gnawing at her, and she wanted to return the favor. If Blake and Alice knew what Sawyer had there, they'd be able to shut him down. Not just that center, but everything. It linked to his legal name. To global holdings.

So far, despite Alice's threat to burn it all to the ground, she hadn't done anything. Had she?

He forced his attention back to the name Lisa sent him, but his mind kept wandering. She was right; Alice couldn't be Cat.

But now the thought was in Sawyer's head, it wouldn't leave. What did he need to put in place, to make sure Tampa was safe, without alerting anyone to the fact that he was worried?

Chapter Twenty-One

Blake never trained for this. There was no experience in his life that prepared him for what he was going through.

Top of his class in sniper school, general for a major crime syndicate, double agent deep undercover for seven years, and now he was stuck waiting in hotel rooms while someone else did the work. He wasn't going to pace today. He'd sit on the bed and watch TV and wait patiently.

Reagan had gone to the bank to check out Alex's safe deposit box. As tame an action as a person could take. Unless there was an armed robbery, but that would be as ludicrous as six gunmen holding up a masquerade ball of Nashville's elite.

Blake banished the rambling thoughts before they could become irrational. He didn't need to be that person. There were too many cameras where Reagan was. Too great a risk of him showing up in some facial-recognition database somewhere. It made sense for him to stay here.

He needed something to do, though. His mind

wasn't built for hiding while other people did the heavy lifting. He looked at the TV. When did the daytime talk-shows start?

He hated this shit.

He flipped through channels, registering none of what he saw.

The room phone rang, the loud bells shattering the unfocused bubble around him. He glared at the device, daring it to make the noise again. It complied.

He could ignore it. Take the receiver off the hook. What if it was Reagan? She'd call the phone she left him. Burner phone. Untraceable.

Unless she couldn't. *Fuck.* He answered. "Yeah."

"How's lapdog life?" Queen's familiar voice jarred him worse than the ringing had.

"Swell. Better than swell. Hell—it's the best." He moved around the room, figuring out what needed to be disposed of, what could be left behind, and what came with him.

It was a short list—he and Reagan lived light. He balanced the phone between his shoulder and his ear, and leveled his gun at the door.

"You're an easy guy to track down." Her tone was conversational. "Sometimes I think you're the worst thing that ever happened to that girl."

The implication that Reagan was in more danger with him than without him gnawed at his joints. "I'm pretty sure her brother was, but you're welcome to your opinion."

"Watch yourself." A growl leaked into Queen's voice.

Note to self—sore spot. "Okay?"

"In case you're wondering if someone is about to burst through the door, we're not." Her pleasantness returned. "From what I can tell, we don't need to be there."

Instinct wanted him to put down the phone and get out of here. Morbid curiosity and the knowledge Queen wasn't as off her rocker as her boss kept him on the line. "I don't believe you, but go on," he said.

"The night of the masquerade, do you remember us talking about Cheshire Cat?"

"I do." He'd brushed it aside as insignificant—another of Jabberwock's deceptions—considering Cat didn't exist.

"Cat is real."

The words clawed up his spine, filling him with a dread he didn't think a simple phrase could evoke. "Why are you really calling?" He kept his question cool.

"Because for the duration of this conversation, and depending on how you react, you're not the enemy. Consider this a professional courtesy."

"In other words, there's something in it for you."

"Yup." Her smirk was audible. "It works like this—Cat tends to have a good bead on where you and Alice are, and a habit of leaking your information whenever the two of you are apart. Cat is a hindrance to you and me, and you're closer to the source right now."

He looked down the sights of his pistol and

tensed, ready to pull the trigger the moment the door burst open. "How close?"

"Is she with you as we speak?"

"Who?" Cat was a *she*? It made as much sense as anything. Did Queen mean Reagan? Pieces tried to fit together, and he refused to let them. He was missing something, but that wasn't it.

Queen sighed. "I'll stop being coy and vague. You're off your game. Jabberwock's got evidence that supports it. Alice is Cheshire Cat."

The statement sank like a stone, weighing down Blake's gut, despite his internal argument that Queen was full of shit. She never said she thought it was true, but that was part of the game—one of the rules of being Jabberwock's representative. She didn't have opinions of her own; she recited his gospel.

"Thanks for the heads-up," he said.

"*Blake.*"

"Nope. We're done. I'll see you when you get here, since I assume you're close." He clicked the receiver, to make sure the line disconnected, then left the phone off the hook.

That wasn't the biggest mindfuck he'd seen come out of Jabberwock's camp, but it was pretty fucking good. And ten million times more likely a way to screw with him than Reagan being Cat. Dragging out a twisted game was Jabberwock's fetish, not hers.

The moment she got back, they needed to move.

Seventeen minutes later, Reagan called, "It's me," through the door before unlocking it and pushing it open. She held a plastic box, and a smile tugged at her lips.

"Keys." He barked the word.

Her glee vanished, and she complied without question, falling into step beside him. They left the hotel in the background and drove. He didn't ask for directions or tell her they were headed east, because of time limits. That was the only thing that held him back.

"How serious is it?" she asked when they hit the freeway.

His every sense was on alert. "Got a call from Queen. In the room." He darted his gaze between the rear window and the road. Within ten minutes, they'd be in a remote enough location he could tell if anyone was following them.

"Tell me what I need to do, when I need to do it."

He spared her a grateful glance. Focus was paramount. Which meant concentrating on the road rather than on the nagging reminder Reagan pitted him against Hare once before. Seattle was a different circumstance, but she was also a different person.

What the fuck was wrong with him, that he was letting this get under his skin? This was the real reason Queen told him anything—to cast a wall of distrust between Blake and Reagan. He wouldn't fall for it and he wouldn't draw any parallels to the fact that, twice now, someone discovered him while she was gone.

The heavy air in the car lifted, the longer they drove. When they stopped for gas, two hundred miles from their original destination, they traded cars with a guy who thought the battered Subaru was *epic and retro.*

They arrived in Green Bay an hour and a half later. He didn't like settling down here, but they needed a direction.

"What happened?" Reagan asked when they were settled in a room.

He should give her the details, laugh them off with her, and move on. But no reason to burden her if it wasn't true. "Like I said, I got a call. I figure she was screwing with my head, but…"

"I know. Can't take any chances." She set down the plastic box. She hadn't let go of it for more than a few seconds since she returned from the bank.

He nodded at her prize. "Should I ask what you found?"

A flicker of her earlier joy returned, hesitation lying underneath, and she unlatched the lid. "It's a bunch of old stuff of Alex's." She held up a stack of photos, then set it aside at the edge of the box, to grab a G.I. Joe doll and a Barbie covered with ink designs. "This is Allie. He popped her head off and smooshed it when I was little, and I was so furious at him." Her voice cracked.

She clenched her jaw. "I worked so hard to give her all these tattoos, and he broke her."

"She has a head now." Blake tried to add a lilt to his voice.

"I noticed." Reagan wiggled it off, and something rattled. She shook the head opening over her palm, and a micro SD card dropped into her hand.

Well, wasn't that convenient? "What's on it?" An edge crept into his voice without his permission.

"I grabbed the box, I glanced inside, and I brought it back to the hotel. Then we ran. I've had as much of a chance to look at this as you have." She studied him for a minute. "Are you all right?"

"Stressed."

"Understandable."

The harder he tried to shove his doubts aside, the louder they raged in his head. He hated this. "Did you have any problems at the bank?"

"Nope. In and out. I had the key and the ID I needed. No big deal."

"Why did we go to the party in Nashville?" he asked.

She frowned. "I told you."

"No. You gave me a vague excuse about Alex sending you there, just like in Minnesota." *Back down.* He struggled to listen to the voice of reason, but it wasn't working. The more he nudged, the more holes he found in her story—all the pieces that hadn't quite fit since he found her again.

"I did it to fuck with Jabberwock's head. It was stupid. It was childish. I wish we hadn't gone. Is that what you're looking for?" The irritation in her voice grew with each sentence.

"No. Because it's not true. Why were we in Nashville? Why did we attend the masquerade? And where did you go the next morning?"

She clenched her jaw and stared at him, ice radiating from her. "I went to call the NSA and tell them where you were. *Not.* You're pushing for something, and I don't know what it is, but I'd like to remind you that you were never part of my plan. I didn't ask you to find me. I didn't ask you to leave Salt Lake with me."

He didn't like how she nailed his suspicions with the flippant retort. "Just tell me what we're doing."

"I am. I have been."

"But you're leaving out details. Let's start simple. What. Was. In Nashville?"

"No. Screw you and this third-degree. I don't know what I did or what Queen said to you, but I thought you and I were good. We moved past this. When I say I trust you with my life, that's literal. I'm not answering your questions, because I don't know why it's so important all the sudden."

"How about a different question?" He yanked his anger and hurt and rage and stowed them under the callousness that would get him through this. "Are you Cheshire Cat?"

She dropped the dolls, and her face paled. "What?"

Chapter Twenty-Two

The answer to Blake's question was simple. It sat on the tip of Reagan's tongue. Say it, and this deescalated, and she could shove *I told you so* back in his face.

But the venom in his voice and that he believed she was Cheshire Cat enough to tear into her like this, made her bite back the truth until it ached in her lungs. She blinked away the sting in her eyes and glared at him. "We were in Nashville, and I was out that morning, because that was where the key was for the safe deposit box. And yes, Alex mentioned Hare, Dormouse, and White Rabbit attended the masquerade every year. You probably don't get this, but I needed that confirmation that my brother wasn't the struggling, starving man I thought he was. I had to see for myself that an event like that, where it was all riches and wealth, was a part of his life."

"Bullshit." Blake spat the word.

The ache inside swelled, and she bit the inside of her cheek. "If you're not going to believe anything I say, why are we having this conversation?"

"If it's true, why not tell me that up front?"

"You want the list?" She was falling for him. Of all the stupid, naive, immature things she'd done to date, that had moved to the top of the list. "I'll count it down. I didn't know why you approached me in Salt Lake, so that seemed like a bad time to give you all the details. Would you have agreed to the party if you knew I just wanted to look? Why the hell did you agree anyway, if you thought it was a bad idea? And because ever since you came back into my life, you look at me like I'm a broken toy, and I didn't want to give you another reason to do that."

"Hang on," she said, as more of the meaning in his accusation sank in. "You think *I* hired people to shoot at us. At me. Even if I'm as far gone as the pity in your eyes says, why the fuck would I do that? What's wrong with you?"

"I don't know." His retort lacked strength. "What's wrong with you, walking back into the middle of all of this, to chase a phantom? We were out. He didn't know where you were."

"*There's nothing wrong with me,*" she shouted. She clenched her jaw until she could draw some of the rage from her voice. It gouged a hole in her chest, to hear him speak to everything she feared was cracked inside. "I don't know why you think it's your job to save me. I didn't ask for that. I don't want that. You look at me and see a little girl who doesn't know anything, who almost got herself killed. I'm not her. Stop trying to heal me or fix me or put me back together. I'm good the way I am."

Except that she wasn't fine, or she wouldn't

be here, but—God damn it—that wasn't his call to make.

"That's not what this is." The accusation was gone from his tone, replaced with something sadder.

She didn't care. "What is it, then? Explain it slow, so I get it."

"You can't sink into the darkness that comes with this world. Seeing it… You can't take that back. Understanding it? Knowing how to navigate it? Necessary evils. But you can't let it become a part of you."

Great. Now she was being lectured. "And you avoided it? That's why you're so well adjusted? Why we spent all this time together, and all it took for you to question me was a phone call and what one of his people said?"

"No." He shook his head. "I'm already a part of it, and it sucks here. I want out. But if you can't climb up from the pit, I don't stand a chance."

"It's a sweet sentiment. Pretty words. It doesn't change the fact you don't trust me."

Blake sank into a chair with a sigh. "Because I still don't get it. I understand the drive and obsession. I wish I didn't, but enough of me gets it that I can't argue it. I don't know why you keep taunting him, though. Las Vegas. Nashville. What does that do?"

She gave a bitter laugh. "You should know that. Queen just did it to you. You spent seven years working for the guy. How is this a mystery?" From where she sat, it was the most obvious thing there was about Jabberwock.

"Explain it slow, so I get it."

She didn't appreciate having her words tossed back at her. "I don't *keep taunting him*. Twice. That was more than enough for me and for him."

"Enough of what?"

"To make him question everything. He's a paranoid bastard. He plays so many games and twists so many things around, he forgets what's real, and he assumes everyone else around him is doing the same." She glared. "And apparently he's right on some counts."

Blake had the good sense to wince.

"The rest of the time, I've stayed as far from him as I could while still doing this." She needed to calm down. Letting her rage and irritation speak brought them here. It may have kept them alive, but it immersed her in a toxic, terrifying game.

She forced a steady rhythm through her veins. "After I left you, and even before, I was furious. When I told Jabberwock I wanted to burn it all down, I meant it as literally as was possible. I climbed back from that ledge. I figured out what Alex left for me, and I spent several months putting it all together. I'm close, and I needed Jabberwock looking in another direction."

"Close to what?"

She nodded at the plastic box that held the dolls. "Assembling the information to publish to the internet. To put everything about him out there. To tell the world who he is and who his clients and vendors are, and to take away every shred of anonymity and leverage he has."

"Until he comes after you," Blake said.

She'd thought of that. The nightmares woke

her. She'd tell Blake the same thing she tried to convince herself of. "He was coming after me anyway. And for all I know, the result would be the same, regardless. This way, his resources are gone, I'll be out of reach when the information is published, and he'll have to find me before someone finds him."

"It's nuts. The entire thing." Blake dropped his face into his hands and rested his elbows on his knees.

It was. But it didn't matter how often she told herself that same thing; she couldn't stop. "I tried to walk away. I can't leave this, given what I know about him. About everything. You came back."

"For you."

She wouldn't let him use her as an excuse. Refused to. "That might be what you told yourself—and that little girl in me that you want to save? She likes that answer—but you're here because you can't walk away."

He clenched his fist then wriggled his fingers, then repeated the gesture. "Can I say *it's both*?"

"Sure. Still think I'm Cat?"

"No. And I didn't before, but I let Queen get in my head, and I needed answers. I'm sorry."

"That's what they do. You've played that game." She tried to put emphasis on her words without letting too much of her hurt show. "You should have asked, instead of…" She frowned. "And I should have told you days ago what I was up to. I'm sorry too. Are we good?"

"We're not. We're better—more honest about the parts that aren't great—but we're far from *good*.”

The words hurt as much as anything he could have said, but she had no argument. “That's fair. I need to get to Logan. Are you still in?”

“We're going back to Utah?” He looked at her in disbelief.

“We have to. It's where we'll find the decryption information for the card.”

He rolled his shoulders and met her gaze. “I'm in. Because you're one hundred percent right about one thing—I can't walk away from this, either.”

She gave him a weak smile, though his confession did anything but reassure her.

Chapter Twenty-Three

Sawyer had no trouble locating his target when he stepped into the Seattle diner. Tony Harrison—Blake's old boss—was one of only four patrons in the local spot at three in the afternoon.

Exactly what Sawyer hoped for. He'd found information that the man came here for a late lunch, specifically to get away from people.

He approached Tony and took the seat next to him at the counter.

Tony glanced sideways but not up. "Plenty of other seats in here, pal. Don't you dare offer to buy me a drink."

"I'll do one better." Sawyer like the blunt attitude. He waved down the waitress. "His lunch is on me." When she was gone, he reached in his jacket pocket and set his phone to record the conversation. An old habit that served him on several occasions.

Tony jerked his head up and swiveled in his seat. "Listen, asshole—" His eyes grew wide when he saw Sawyer. "I know you."

"And we've never even been formally introduced. I'm flattered."

"You're the Hare."

"Just *Hare*. It's a name, not a title." Sawyer grabbed a nearby packet of sugar and rolled it between his fingers. Looking at the vein poking out on the side of Tony's neck, he decided telling him he was actually Jabberwock might end the conversation sooner than he wanted.

Tony reached under his jacket, and Sawyer grabbed his wrist. "Hear me out," Sawyer said. "We have a mutual problem."

"You nearly cost me my career." Tony strained against his grip, then twisted free with a grunt.

"No. Blake Allen and Reagan Lidell could cost you your career. As I said, *mutual problem.*"

Tony narrowed his eyes, then turned back to his meal. "Talk to me." He sawed off a bit of steak, dragged it through egg yolk, then shoved the forkful in his mouth.

Sawyer was surprised it didn't take more convincing. This was only a foot in the door, though. "If I point you to them, can you do the rest?"

"Why would you do that?"

Mutual problem should have covered that. Sawyer was losing interest in the conversation. "They're making business difficult."

"I bet. And not my problem." Tony snorted. "I'd have loved to nab you at the same time we took Ms. Lidell, but no. You and your cohorts were off-limits. Jabberwock was the priority."

"Lucky me. What *did* happen when you grabbed her, anyway?"

"Complete fluke. We lost her in Salt Lake,

and the higher-ups were furious. Then we get an anonymous tip—*from a cat*, of all things—that she was holed up in a condo here. We kept eyes on the place for a few days, and we were ready to scale back our people, when she stormed out in the middle of the night."

Sawyer hid his frown. Did Alice call them? They extracted her, so it made sense. "So, you took her to a safe house, and she refused to cooperate?" It was something he'd been curious about. Why didn't she tell them that one piece of information about him? She gave him reasons, but it felt like there was more he didn't know.

"*Safe house*. Yeah." Another snort, followed by Tony slicing off another piece of steak. "We've got a *holding facility*"—he made air quotes—"where we introduced her to a taste of what *held indefinitely* can mean."

"Oh?" Sawyer would say as little as possible if it meant this man kept talking.

"The bitch fucking hated it. Screamed. Threatened. Negotiated. She burned herself, to get attention."

Sawyer liked a good game, but the glee in Tony's voice sent fury racing through his veins. Locking someone in a room wasn't a game; it was a zoo. "I bet." His voice was thin. "I've got what I need. I'll be in touch."

"Looking forward to it." Tony set down his silverware, wiped his fingers on a napkin, and extended his hand.

In a fluid motion, Sawyer grabbed the knife, twisted his arm, and plunged it into the other man's throat. He spun and walked from the diner, leaving a chorus of terrified screams behind him. A tiny smile played on his face, and satisfaction flitted inside. Alice didn't deserve to be locked in a cage. A maze perhaps, but only as a chance to play with her.

He checked the ground, to ensure he wasn't tracking any bloody footprints. The splatter on his face and arm were the worst of it. He climbed into the car waiting for him a few yards from the entrance. "Back to the hotel," he said to the driver.

Less than half an hour later, he let himself into Lisa's room. She was sitting on her bed, her attention on her laptop. She didn't look up. "Did you have fun on your play date?"

"It had its ups and downs, but overall was a success." He had an idea now what to do, to get under Alice's skin. He knew Cat had been tracking him for a while, though he still didn't know if it was her.

But if he talked to more of Blake's former colleagues, he could come up with the perfect way to end this game with Blake and Alice. It would start with a cage, because only he was allowed to put her in one, but she wouldn't stay there for long. She had to be given a fair chance. "Did I miss anything interesting?" he asked.

"Yes."

"Ooh." He settled on the mattress and stretched his legs out next to hers. "I didn't expect that." The image on her screen was a traffic-camera view of an interstate. "What's that?"

"Blake and Alice." She switched windows to a still shot and pointed to a sedan near the top right corner of the image. "This is the car they traded for in Wisconsin, on I-80 in Cheyenne, heading west. It was taken thirty minutes ago." She tabbed to another photo. "This is them, getting in that car in Lincoln Nebraska, a few hours earlier."

"I like it when you tell stories." He grinned.

"This is a good one. They're going to Logan."

Sawyer's amusement wilted. "Why would they do that?"

"Reag—Alice was born there. Alex lived there."

He was missing something, but the buildup made the wait worth it. "And…?"

"Alex bought that house years ago. That's where Alice is going. I'm not one hundred percent certain, but I'm pretty sure."

"How do you know he bought it?" Something like that should have showed up on the records Sawyer kept—alerts and tracking he had in place, to let him know if any of Alex's assets became active.

Lisa met his gaze, her amusement gone. "He told me."

"And you never thought it was important to share that with me?" The annoyance Sawyer felt in the diner returned, nibbling at his senses.

"He asked me not to, and I held onto it until I realized you needed know. My loyalty is to you. But this chase… The call you had me make to Blake a few days ago, though I don't think for a second that she's Cat… It's all falling apart, and you're letting it." Irritation dragged through her voice.

"Stop. Breathe."

"No, God damn it. Listen to me. Pay attention to something other than your own fucking obsession for a few minutes. Fuck—for all I know, you're Cheshire Cat, and this is a new game I don't understand, and you've gone that far off the deep end with your self-sabotage."

He thought he was doing well with Lisa. Showing her what she needed to see, to keep her happy. He'd try harder. "I'm sorry. And I'm not Cat."

"Do you swear? Promise me by anything our friendship and business relationship ever meant to you?"

He drew an *X* over his chest. "Cross my heart. What can I do to make this better?"

She sighed and rubbed the back of her neck. "I have the plane ready to take us to the Logan airport. But after that, you need to step back from Alice. I'm not saying ignore her, but your focus needs to change."

"Of course." He gave her a warm smile. This was better. He and Lisa were good again. The way it should be. "One more game, and then I'll take a few steps back."

Chapter Twenty-Four

It was after eleven at night when Reagan and Blake drove down the mountain pass and toward the small grouping of lights in the center of the valley. It wasn't as cold here as Illinois or Wisconsin, but seven or minus seven, it meant frozen fingers either way. He rolled his neck and blinked, to restore moisture to his eyes, but they'd dried out hours ago.

As a sign came into view, promising a chain motel with a number in the name, he navigated to the off ramp.

"This isn't our exit," Reagan said. "The address is five miles east." Those were the most words she'd said to him in a single block since the argument in Wisconsin.

That didn't make them any more reassuring. "And it'll still be there in the morning," he said. They'd driven straight through, trading off who slept and who drove. It made the trip go faster, and offered another excuse for them to not speak.

He didn't know how to repair the chasm he created with his accusation. No matter how deep he dug in his brain, he couldn't find an answer. The powerless feeling was made worse by the looming cloud he swore followed them since they got on the road—that nagging feeling they didn't have a lot of time, period.

"I want to go tonight. I'll drive the rest of the way, if you're too tired." Reagan's sarcasm was interrupted by her yawn.

He forced aside the irritation that came with exhaustion. "Do you know what you're looking for?"

"No. But I will when I see it. That's the way it's been with everything so far."

"If that's the case, you need to be sharp and rested." He turned down the street leading to the motel.

"I'd like to see it now."

And he wanted to climb into bed and sleep. He understood her insistence, though. She was so close to… whatever this was. "Compromise?" he said. "We'll drive by tonight, and go back first thing tomorrow morning, when we've slept, and it's light outside, and there's less of a chance of the neighbors calling the cops on the people traipsing around an abandoned property in the middle of the night.

"All right." She sounded as if it was anything but.

He pointed the vehicle toward the address and followed her directions, turning left here and right there. They reached their destination street. The lights were few and far between, so it was difficult to tell what kind of condition the houses were in, but the architecture dated most of them at more than a century old. They had huge yards—the kind of space developers paid a fortune for, in bigger cities.

"Park over there." She pointed at a two-story with a one car garage, surrounded by trees almost as old as the house. "I just want to take a look."

He didn't even slow down. "No." He winced at the edge in his voice. "Why are you pushing so hard to do this *right now*?"

"What if something happens between today and tomorrow? Don't you feel it?" She sighed. "Never mind."

He didn't know if her sensing the same vibe was a confirmation he wasn't going insane or a warning they should put more faith in. "I do feel it, but we can't do this tonight, for all the reasons I listed."

"You're right." She twisted in her seat, facing the house, as they drove away. She didn't sit forward again until they turned and it was gone from view.

A little while later, they stepped into their new hotel room. He tossed their bags aside with the last bit of care he could muster, and latched the door shut. When he turned to face Reagan, she draped her arms over his shoulders and pressed close.

"I'm too wired to sleep." A seductive, playful note leaked into her tone. "Distract me?"

Electricity slid over his skin, drawing his nerve endings to life but leaving his brain behind. Fuck—she felt good. "No." That ached to say. He extracted himself from the embrace, and stepped around her, moving into the room.

"Why not? Is today different from any other day?"

It was completely different. The understanding struck him and sank in. "Because I care. That is, I cared before—on that basic we're-human-beings level—but I care about you now. If we fuck again, I want it to mean something, and not be an excuse."

"If you're doing this to make a point, you don't have to prove anything to anyone." She rubbed the back of her neck.

"That's not what this is."

"I know you're a good guy, and you should know it too. You've been my white knight, even if you don't think so. Holding me when I need it. Saving me. Everything you've done, because it's who you are, is why I trust you."

She wasn't tossing around the word *trust* lightly. He should have known that, but it meant more this time. "Do you feel the same, even now?" After what he said? The accusations he made?

"Even now."

God, he was an idiot. "I'm sorry. I realize I said it before, but I need to reinforce that I mean it. I shouldn't have listened to Queen. I let the situation get to me and screw with my head. If we get out of this—"

"*When.*"

His smile took more energy than it should. "*When* this is over, the secrets have to stop. We both have our reasons, but I should have given you the same faith you did me."

"You see a future for us at the end of this?" The corners of her eyes tugged up.

He'd said that, didn't he? "I don't know how far it'll go, but yeah, I'd like to see what's there. Outside this twisted realm of madness."

"Me too."

"In that case, at least come up with a better excuse for sex than *distract me*." Blake slid a hint of teasing into his voice. "Something more like *in case this is our last night on Earth*."

She rolled her eyes and laughed. "Wow. That's depressing. How about we strip out all the excuses, do what comes naturally, and enjoy each other's company?"

"That's a plan I can't argue with." He tugged her to sit on the bed with her back to his chest, and wrapped his arms around her waist. He kissed along the back of her neck and down to her shoulder. "I'm serious about wanting sleep, though. Christ—I want you, but I'm old and tired."

"All right. We'll sleep." Reagan extracted herself long enough to shed all her clothes except her T-shirt and panties.

He stripped down to his boxers, pulled back the comforter, and climbed into bed. When she lay next to him and pulled his arm over her, a filter of comfort muted the lingering sense of *something bad*.

This felt right. Different than before—not like he was protecting her, like it was a more equal arrangement—but still right.

Despite the exhaustion searing through him and weighing down his limbs, tension kept his gaze fixed on the clock on the nightstand. The numbers clicked up the minutes, toward an hour.

"You're not sleeping either?" Reagan asked.

"Nope."

"This sucks."

He glided his fingers down her arm, to dance

them over her hip. "Perhaps a distraction is a good idea after all."

"Did you have something specific in mind?" She pressed back into him, and tilted her head so she met his gaze.

Each time she shifted against him, it chased away more of the shadows and drew his desire closer to the surface. "Very specific." He dipped under the elastic of her underwear, to tease her bare skin, but didn't move lower.

"Like what?" Her teasing question evaporated in a sigh when he brushed the crease where hip met thigh.

His cock hardened. How would things have gone between them, if they'd met without the specter of Jabberwock surrounding them? Would they have clicked? Not what he wanted to be thinking about. He dipped lower and slid between her folds. The tiny gasp that slipped from her throat was like a spark dancing through him.

"Pressing this button here"—he drew a tight circle around her clit—"and sliding inside you to see what happens next." He dipped into her opening. She grew wetter with each new movement, making it easy for him to slip along his path.

She clenched around his fingers, then pumped her hips to the steady pace he set. "Then what?" Her question was strained.

"Greedy girl. Isn't that enough?" Blake dragged his lips along her neck, before pausing to suck on the soft flesh. The scent of winter clung to her skin, mingling with the soap from their last hotel.

He slipped out of her and moved back to her

clit again, tracing and nudging. Teasing in time with her moans and the thrust of her hips.

"It's good. It's fantastic." Her words were punctuated by gasps. "But it feels like there's a Part Two."

"There could be." And would be, if he was lucky. His erection was so hard it ached, begging for release. He wanted to prolong this moment—stay locked in this cloud that was only them. "Have to finish Part One first."

He increased the speed and pressure on her sex, circling faster the more she ground into his touch. She gripped his arm, digging in her fingers, but didn't try to pull him way. Each new gasp was intoxicating, and the feeling of her heat on his skin, wet and desperate, filled his head.

He recognized the sound of her nearing climax. The pauses when she held her breath. The whimpers when she let go. They tightened across his nerves, making him wish his dick was buried inside her.

When she came, she bucked under his touch, before pulling him away with a low laugh. She raised his hand and drew a finger into her mouth. When she traced her tongue along the pad, licking off her juices, his cock twinged with envy.

He tilted his head to nip her earlobe. "Fuck. I want to be inside you."

"There *is* a Part Two." She wiggled her ass.

He nudged her shoulder blades forward and repositioned himself for a better angle. When he fisted his shaft, a spike of desire lit his senses up. He found the sense to grab a condom from his wallet and roll it on.

He moved her leg, pushed aside her panties, and nudged her opening. He thrust inside without hesitation, and she arched her back. The sensation froze his tongue, so he could only manage a grunt. Wittiness evaporated. She was tight and slick, wrapped around him. Driving back into him. Milking him.

"I can't— *Jesus.* You feel incredible." Saying that much took more of his focus than he wanted.

He found the swollen bud between her legs. She jerked away, then eased back into his attention. He couldn't hold out long like this. The weight of the last several days had faded into the background, leaving him with only the scents and sounds and sensations of *now*. He needed this release.

"I want you to come again," he murmured against her skin. "Pinch your nipples."

She nodded, and shoved her shirt aside to grab her breast. The hint of skin, smooth and pale in the glint of moonlight peeking through the curtains, was an invisible vise, squeezing in his gut and tightening in his balls.

He buried his face in her neck, but the scent didn't help. Nipping, sucking, then biting the tender skin, he elicited a drawn-out groan from her. Everything seemed to pause for a heartbeat, then she cried out when she came, clenching around his cock.

It was like someone flicked a switch. He spilled inside her, pounding hard and fast, grasping her hip. He thrust until he was spent, then slowed to a stop.

She scooted closer again, and he held on tight.

"Better?" she asked, sleep tinging her question.

"Much." His eyes were tugging shut. He found enough presence of mind to dispose of the condom, then draped his arm around Reagan again. "Sleep now?"

She nodded. "And tomorrow, when we have what we need, it'll all be over. In a week, we'll celebrate Thanksgiving on an island, thousands of miles from here, and put the bad parts of this behind us."

"We absolutely will." He wouldn't clarify which part of her statement he was agreeing with. Pretending this was almost over felt like as big a lie as any of them.

Chapter Twenty-Five

Reagan stepped from the car and paused for half a second with her shoes inches from the ground. An odd splash of fear spilled through her, as though stepping on the sidewalk would make the house vanish.

"You all right?" Blake called from where he stood, several feet up the front walk.

She shook the odd impulse aside. "I'm good." She joined him and took a long look around the front yard. Snow covered the browning grass in patches. The lawn that poked through didn't look overgrown. Did someone take care of this place?

"Do you want to start out here?" Blake asked.

"I don't think he'd leave it exposed to the elements like that, but we'll check out here as a last resort." Her pulse thrummed in her ears, and she couldn't shake the dread that encased her.

She unlocked the front door with a key she'd recovered in Tampa Bay. The little girl in her wanted to believe Alex hid them all over the country to give her more of a challenge. To make the game more fun. She suspected it was to keep someone from stumbling on the pieces and knowing how to connect them.

She stepped into the home, expecting a rush of… something. The same cold air that was outside greeted her from the inside. Boards creaked under her, as she crossed the hardwood floor, but she left no footprints behind. A brush of the curtains hanging over frost-covered windows didn't send dust fluttering to the ground. Someone was doing basic maintenance on the place.

She heard a soft *click* behind her, followed by several more, and turned to see Blake flipping a light switch by the door up and down. "No power. Not that I expected it."

"I guess you were smart to make me wait until it was light outside." Reagan gave him a tight smile.

"I won't even say, *I told you so*."

She looked around. There was no furniture, but the living room was big enough for a couch, a few chairs, and a small TV. Nothing in here was familiar. She expected a gnawing wave of nostalgia, but she wasn't even a year old when they moved out of the place.

Did Alex love it here? He must have felt some attachment, to be compelled to buy it.

Nothing caught her eye. The walls were painted eggshell, and the trim stained dark. She wandered into the kitchen. The cabinets matched the walnut-colored wood. Power outlets and empty caves sat where appliances should be. She looked in each cupboard, shining her light into all the corners, but there were no uneven seams or cracks. Nothing that looked out of place.

When she turned back to the doorway leading to the living room, Blake stood just inside. He moved out of her way, and she headed upstairs.

She was grateful he kept his distance and had nothing to say, but at the same time, it was reassuring to have him there. An eerie creeping sensation traveled with her, as she worked her way from room to room, as if someone was watching.

No one was here but Blake.

Several hours later, she'd been through the house top to bottom several times. Nothing was familiar. Clouds had moved in, blocking the afternoon light and casting the house in shadows, so she had to strain, to see.

Their light would have evaporated soon anyway, with the short days. She sat on the top stair and dropped her face into her hands.

Blake settled next to her, his shoulder pressing against hers. "What do you want to do?"

"I don't know." She tried to keep the frustration from her voice. She'd knocked on walls, to listen for hollow sounds. Looked for hidden latches. Anything. Did she read Alex's clues wrong, or was whatever he left gone already?

"We can't do much else today." Blake's voice was kind. "Do you want to try again tomorrow? We'll grab food, go back to the hotel, and watch stupid movies."

She didn't know what good coming back tomorrow would do them, but stubbornness had gotten her this far. "Sounds like a plan."

When they returned the next day, she brought with her almost everything she'd collected from Alex's scavenger hunt.

She wandered through the house, not processing any of it. Where was she supposed to start? What did she miss yesterday?

"I'll do another look downstairs," Blake said.

She nodded and headed up to the bedrooms. She walked into one with pale-blue walls. Emptiness stared back at her, washing over her with the futility of it all. She dropped the box of Alex's stuff and slid to the floor with her back against the wall. "What do you want me to find?" she asked the room.

She pulled the box closer and grabbed the stack of photos off the top. Unlike the digital ones that started her search, these were on yellowed paper, the colors faded. There were a couple of her and Alex on her first day of kindergarten—him with his arm around her shoulder, and her wearing a giant grin.

More of him riding a bike… Her playing with the family dog… Her thoughts trailed off as she stared at the print in her hand.

It was Alex when he was about seven, standing next to a crib with a baby in it. *Me.* Alex was pointing at baby-Reagan. There was a window to the side, a giant tree showing through the glass.

She looked between the photo and the window in front of her. The tree out there was barren where the one in the photo was covered in leaves, but it was the same tree. She was certain of it.

"*Blake.*" She looked between the image and

the room. What was she supposed to see?

"Be right there," he called.

In the photo, the wall was papered with cowboys and dinosaurs, rather than painted blue. She looked closer. Alex *wasn't* pointing at her. There was a stick-figure drawing on the wall above her head. She pushed to her feet and crossed to look at the wall in that same general area.

The faint outline of cowboys peeked through thin paint, and there was a tiny bubble in the finish. She picked at it, and the wallpaper underneath tore.

Who the fuck painted over wallpaper? And did such a shitty job? She didn't care. Her pulse hammered in her ears and her excitement grew. *"Blake."*

She tore at the wallpaper. Where the hell was Blake?

An envelope wrapped in plastic fluttered to the ground. She bent at the waist, snagged it, and tore away the wrapping, forcing herself to go slow, so as not to tear anything inside.

A stack of bearer bonds was nestled in there. She flipped through the notes. There had to be thousands of dollars' worth. Her thumb skipped over a different texture, and she paused.

She went back to the obstruction and pulled out another photo. This was a Polaroid, and much newer. More vibrant. She swore her heart stopped when she saw the image. It was Alex and Queen, both smiling, arms around each other. On the bottom of the print, it read *My Kitten*.

Reagan shoved the image into the envelope, and her gut sank into her shoes. Pieces collided in her head, leaving a dull throb behind her eyes. Was Queen the woman Alex talked about with so much adoration in his notes? Why else would he leave this here? With that inscription?

"*Blake*." She turned and almost collided with Jabberwock. Her voice stuck in her throat.

"Blake is busy." Jabberwock gave her a smile that made her want to sink into the floor and vanish. "You and I need to talk."

"I'm not in the mood for a game." Could she get around him before he grabbed her?
He shot his hand toward her throat and pushed her back, digging his palm into her jugular as he used his longer reach and body weight to pin her to the wall. "Too bad. I let you go six months ago because you said we could play a game. We're going to play."

Chapter Twenty-Six

Blake was in the kitchen, rapping on cabinet doors, when Reagan called his name. She sounded excited.

"Be right there," he shouted. He stepped into the living room, and the floor creaked behind him. He reached for his gun as he whirled, but something sharp jabbed him in the neck. A needle? Pain seared through the muscle, and the edges of his vision blurred.

"I'm so sorry about this," Queen said, before his world went black.

Blake's head was screaming, starting with the stabbing pain in his neck and spreading to his temple.

No. That wasn't his head making the noise. It was coming from outside his skull. Did he fall asleep with the TV on? He tried to pry his eyes open, but the lids felt like they were weighted with cement.

He waded through the fog in his brain, to remember what happened. Reagan was shouting for him, because they were in the house. He couldn't grasp anything after that. It was a black cloud. He'd been drugged? By whom?

The screaming was louder, hammering his ears until he winced. It was Reagan. Was she shouting for him? No. She sounded terrified.

"Don't you dare do this to me, you fucker." Her voice was sharp, bordering on panic. *"Don't ignore me, you fucking asshole."*

Blake forced himself toward consciousness, and his surroundings swam into view. It was a small room, and he lay in the corner, on a futon. Reagan stood at the door, pounding on it with her fists.

He struggled to stand, whatever was in his system receding more with each movement. The room was similar, but not identical, to the one Reagan had been locked in so many months ago.

He reached her and wrapped her in a hug from behind, pinning her arms to her sides. "Stop." He slurred the word.

"Don't touch me." She broke away and spun to face him.

He stumbled back but regained his footing quickly. "Help me out. Tell me what happened." It would fill in the blanks for him, but it would also force her to access parts of her mind not attached to the panic driving her.

"It's Jabberwock." She said the name with a combination of disgust and fear. Her voice was raw but strong. She hadn't been screaming *too* long.

Not Blake's former employers then. He didn't know if he was relieved or a little more nervous. "How long have we been in here?" He approached her again and clasped her wrists loosely.

This time she didn't break away. "Probably

only ten or fifteen minutes. And the drive was another fifteen or so."

"So we're still in Logan." He examined her hands. The fleshy sides were pink and swollen, starting to bruise. She must have been hammering as hard as she was yelling. The skin wasn't broken, though.

"You are indeed not far from where we found you." Jabberwock's voice crackled through the air. It sounded as though it was being filtered through a screen before spitting out of the speakers. "I didn't have the luxury of a fully armed contingent to help me snag you, and I was concerned, Blake, that if we pumped too many sedatives through your system, it might do damage before we got started."

Fantastic. But not even remotely.

"What's the game?" Reagan asked.

This was bullshit. "We're not playing any games." Blake looked around. The speaker was in a corner above the bed. It looked like a squashed metal cone.

"You're not in a position to negotiate." Jabberwock's reply screeched with feedback.

Blake pressed his palm to the wall and dragged his hand enough to get a feel for the texture. Painted brick or cinder block.

His coat had been removed, as well as his gun and holster. Not that he was surprised. He reached for his ankle out of habit.

"I took them all," Jabberwock said. "I want to have some fun; I'm not stupid."

There were cameras too. Blake wasn't surprised. Where were they? An old school, maybe.

An abandoned warehouse or restaurant.

Reagan crossed her arms. "What's. The. Game?"

"I'm getting to that. Fucking hell. You'd think a woman who hid as well as you did for so long would have a little more patience." Jabberwock's tone was flippant. "I'm telling a story first."

"Fine," Reagan said.

Blake continued to scan the room, but there was as little to see as in Alex's house. Now that the drugs were mostly gone from his system, he could think. Stand without wobbling. Process their surroundings. He'd prefer the headache left as well, but he wasn't betting on that happening any time soon. "You do know I'll kill you as soon as I find you. Bare hands or whatever it takes."

Jabberwock's tinny chuckle filled the room. "I knew you'd play. Here's the thing—it turns out the two of you pissed a lot of people off when you resurfaced as not dead. That wasn't my doing. You can thank Cat, who I thought was Alice, but now I'm not certain. That's not relevant. It didn't take much to find out what happened to Alice after she vanished from my condo.

"We've got a *holding facility*, where we introduced her to a taste of what *held indefinitely* can mean." Tony Harrison—Blake's old boss—sounded like a bad movie villain when the recording played over the speaker. "The bitch fucking hated it. Screamed. Threatened. Negotiated. She burned herself, to get attention."

With each new word, Blake's ire grew another notch toward rage. Reagan clenched her jaw and fists, staring straight ahead.

"Guy was an asshole," Jabberwock said. "He's not a problem anymore. But my point is it was easy to find details. I didn't have a lot of time to reconstruct the room, but you won't be in it long, anyway. A little cash passed to the right people. A few nudges with others. My hell, Blake, your NSA friends were more willing to sell you out than—well—you were us."

"Talking isn't a game." Blake couldn't keep the irritation from his voice.

"Right. Sorry. Let's move on." Jabberwock's exaggerated sigh made the sound system crackle and screech. "There's a Glock G22 under the futon with a single bullet it in."

"You can't play Russian Roulette with a semi-automatic," Reagan said.

Jabberwock laughed. "I did miss you. I'm still explaining the rules. From there, it's simple. Gun is yours. I let you out. If you make it to me with that bullet still in the chamber, you can take your shot, Blake."

There was a catch. Blake didn't doubt for a second this would be much more difficult than that. He might be concerned about a pressure-sensitive trap under the futon, but he'd been lying on it, so his getting up would have changed that weight. Still, he kicked the mattress aside rather than flipping it. Sure enough, in the corner, there was a pistol on the ground.

He approached the weapon with caution, then grabbed it. He knelt on the floor, ejected the chambered round, and field stripped the gun so he could examine the springs, the barrel, the firing pin—all of it.

It appeared to be in order. That Jabberwock had given him a loaded sidearm, regardless of the limited ammunition, overloaded Blake's dread.

"Satisfied?" Jabberwock asked.

Reagan extended her hand, and Blake grabbed it, more for the contact and assurance than for help standing. "No," he said, "but you'd be disappointed if I said otherwise."

"So true." The latch on the door clicked, and it cracked open. "You were anxious for the game? Let's play."

Chapter Twenty-Seven

Reagan should be grateful for the open door, but it made her stomach plummet into her shoes. Blake encircled her waist from behind and buried his face in her hair. The intimacy was nice but ill timed.

"Listen to me." His warm breath hit the back of her neck. His voice was so quiet she had to strain to hear the words. "*Yes* or *no* answers only when I ask. Understand?"

"Yes." She got it—he didn't want to be overheard. This wouldn't be a practical tactic once they left the room, regardless of what waited, but for now, it helped calm her racing pulse.

"I'll take the lead when we walk out of here," he said. "Not that the gun will be much more useful than a club, once I fire it, but I need you to watch our backs."

Of course she would. "Yes."

"Two priorities. Find you a weapon—a stick, something, anything—and get an idea of where we are. Make sense?"

"Yes." She could do this. The conversation was all logical steps she would have figured out on her own, but talking through them helped her segment her thoughts.

"And most important, though you're more familiar with this than I am, we promise each other right now we don't let this guy fuck with our heads. Right?"

"Yes."

"Cuddle time's over. Break it up." Jabberwock's volume made her eardrums throb.

Blake kissed the back of Reagan's neck. "When we get out of here, I can have us on a flight to Fiji in about two hours."

She had to hide her smile. "Yes."

Blake stepped around her.

"Finally." Jabberwock sounded bored.

This wasn't going to get old fast or anything.

Blake nudged open the door, and a siren blared over the speakers. It echoed in her skull and vibrated in her feet and made it impossible to hear what he was saying, despite seeing his lips move.

He frowned and left the room. She willed herself to go with him, but her mind was sucked back into the cell she'd been kept in. The blare of the TV. The bright lights.

She clenched her hand until her nails dug into her palm, and focused on the pain to stay grounded.

There was a light touch on her arm. She'd squeezed her eyes shut? She looked up, to find Blake had returned and was watching her with concern.

She gave him a weak smile, not willing to try to be heard over the noise.

He gestured to the door, and she nodded. The last thing she wanted was to be a liability. She needed to hold herself together.

When she stepped from the room, the noise stopped. The silence that settled in was almost as disconcerting. A look up and down the hallway showed her lockers—some open, some not, some without doors at all—and rooms with closed doors. They were in the condemned high school, outside of town.

"We have to check each door." Blake's whisper in her ear mingled with the echo of ringing.

They approached the first classroom. She tried the knob, while he kept watch. It was locked. From the resistance the door offered when she leaned into it, it was heavy. Probably too sturdy for them to pop it out of its lock.

There was a tall, narrow window, with a wooden board blocking the other side. Even if they could smash the glass, it was too far above the knob, for her to reach the lock. As they moved to the next room, Blake kept his attention on the new territory, and Reagan watched where they'd been. A shiver fell over her and her breath came out in white puffs. In the room they'd been locked in, it was warm.

Out here, the temperature was low enough to remind her it was below freezing outside and their coats had been taken. They both wore heavy hoodies, but those wouldn't keep their fingers warm, or really any of part of them for long.

The approached a locker the door of which hung from a single hinge. Blake handed her the pistol, and she adopted an alert posture. Part of her time over the last several months had been spent practicing with a firearm. She still didn't know that she could fire it, if the situation called for it, but she could hit her target if she pulled the trigger.

A screeching sound made her cringe. Blake was kicking the sheet metal free and prying the bar that acted as a locking mechanism from it. He handed her the makeshift weapon, and she returned his Glock.

There was a stairwell at the end of the hallway, as well as an exit. Heavy double doors blocked both. She leaned into one and then the other with her shoulder. They let in a gust of frigid air, and she caught a glimpse of sunlight and heard the rattle of chains.

She couldn't see any details outside, and they couldn't get to the locks holding the doors in place. But if someone came in through those doors behind them, they'd hear it.

The sirens blared over the speakers the moment she left the landing. Her heart jumped into her throat, threatening to hammer its way free.

Blake glanced between her and their surroundings, his brow furrowed.

She swallowed her desire to curl up in a ball and scream for it to stop, clenching and unclenching her fist until her thoughts were clear. When they started down the next hallway, the sound cut out again.

They repeated the lock checking, then creeped forward, around the entire floor. It was laid out like a square. They found one way out—a doorway leading up one of the staircases.

Blake led the way up. When she climbed, the sirens blared again. She jumped but stayed with

Blake. Within seconds, the sound stopped. She wanted to shout, *I've survived worse, asshole,* but was afraid he'd see it as a challenge.

"I knew they were wrong about you." Jabberwock's casual tone was as grating as the sirens. She was going to hear the bastard in her sleep for years. "At least a couple of Blake's former colleagues insisted they had broken you. That the loud noise would be a surefire trigger. But you're stronger than that, Alice. I never doubted it."

"Do I have to kill myself, to get a person in here?" Her voice mocked her from the PA system, tugging her back toward the past.

She glared at the nearest speaker. "I'll tell you the same thing I told them—I don't know what you fucking want." While she argued with the disembodied voice, she followed Blake through the new floor, repeating the routine they established downstairs—check the door, check behind them, move on.

"Whatever they told you they wanted, they lied," Jabberwock said. "They were trying to break you, but don't worry. Like I said before, Tony is gone. As for what I want? You. I want you to push aside all your preconceived notions and indoctrination about good and bad and right and wrong, and understand you're not restricted by those rules."

"Thanks for the vote of confidence," she muttered, sarcasm dripping from her words.

"You're welcome. But I'll warn you—like with them, if you hurt yourself on purpose, I won't come running." Jabberwock's tone was sad, but it wasn't quite right. It took Reagan a moment to figure out why. It was exaggerated. Insincere. "You're better than that, though. You won't do that again."

She wasn't as convinced as him. Despite the voice in her head, chanting for her to keep going—to push through this—there was a part of her that didn't know if she could. What happened the first time, when she was locked away, tore her down so much that she fought to keep herself calm now.

She refused to surrender or sink into despair. She and Blake could make it through this. Couldn't they?

Chapter Twenty-Eight

Blake could ignore the chill for several hours, as long as he kept moving and stayed focused on the situation. The soldier inside, the instinct that kicked in when there was danger, was torn. He didn't know if he could simultaneously keep an eye on Reagan and pay appropriate attention to their environment.

He glanced at her, in the midst of Jabberwock's most recent string of rambling. She looked rattled—understandable—but she was holding together all right.

He had to trust her to do what was required. *I do*. Admitting it helped him draw in more focus to give the school.

They moved to the next classroom. Jabberwock was herding them. Blake didn't have any illusions about that. He didn't see an alternative, though. It was either proceed or give up and freeze to death. The sun would set in five or six hours, by his estimates, but it would get colder before then.

Reagan jiggled the next doorknob, and something creaked.

Every muscle in Blake's body tensed. He

heard wood splinter and looked up in time to see the ceiling split open. "*Watch out.*" His bark didn't do him any good. One of the timber supports cracked across his right arm.

A howl of pain tore from his throat, and he dropped the gun.

"*Blake.*" The moment the dust cleared, Reagan was by his side.

He nodded at the pistol. "Grab it first."

The speakers crackled to life. "I'm a little concerned your name is such an intrinsic part of her vocabulary," Jabberwock said, "but I am going to admit you're not looking so good, Blake."

Blake tried to move his arm and had to clench his jaw to bite back another scream. He turned his gaze up toward the ceiling. The roof had collapsed, and snow fluttered down on them. They needed to move, and stay close to the walls, in case the damage spread. "Help me stand," he said to Reagan through clenched teeth.

She nodded and—gun in hand—helped him drape his other arm over her shoulder and climb to his feet.

"*God.* I wish I'd planned that." Jabberwock's voice was filled with glee. "It's got most of my plans beat. Is it broken?"

Blake twisted his arm again. "Dislocated, I think," he told Reagan.

She stayed by his side until he was leaning against a bank of lockers. The icy metal bit into his back through his sweatshirt.

She watched him with concern, but the panic was gone from her eyes. "We need to bind it to you somehow. Make it immovable."

"Yes." If he kept it very still and thought about anything else, the pain dialed back to levels that allowed him to think. He wouldn't be able to shoot with that arm. Fortunately, he was trained left-handed too. Not well, but it would do. He held out his good hand. "Gun."

Reagan shook her head. "I've got it."

"Come here." He clasped the back of her neck and pulled her closer. With her ear near his mouth, he whispered, "I'm about to pull what you'll think is a steaming bag of macho bullshit, but it's not. I won't hesitate to pull the trigger. Will you?"

The second-long pause before she said, "No," was all the answer he needed.

"Gun." He held out his hand again.

She surrendered the Glock. "You're about to hate this." Sympathy shone in her eyes. "I did it for Alex once, when he fell on a camping trip." She trailed her fingers down the useless limb hanging at his side.

Blake didn't know if he was relieved that she might know how to reset his shoulder. "Go for—*Fuuuuuuuck*." Another scream tore from his throat when she twisted and yanked the joint back into place without warning.

"Better?" she asked.

"Fuck, no." He struggled to catch his breath. "Okay, maybe a little." It took several seconds, but the stars stopped dancing in front of his eyes.

Jabberwock was silent through the ordeal. *Thank God for small favors.*

Reagan waited until Blake focused on her

again, then nodded down the hallway. She'd changed so much since he first met her, but he'd been wrong before where she had it right. She wasn't broken; she was stronger. More mature. And when they got out of here, he was taking her away from this fucked up system. Someplace they could vanish.

The resumed their hunt-and-peck journey. Pain licked the edges of his consciousness, whispering, *Can you make it? Are you sure?* He forced it back.

Whatever Jabberwock had waiting at the end of this was going to be worse than a dislocated shoulder.

That didn't mean he was going to give up. He didn't work that way. Even when he'd been shot, he didn't let the darkness creep in.

So why was it harder to stash this feeling behind a wall than it should be?

*

Reagan was worried about Blake. His skin was several shades paler than when they arrived. He gripped his pistol tightly and kept up his surveillance, but if he didn't clench his jaw, his teeth chattered. The injury plus the falling temperatures had to be wreaking havoc on his system.

"Fuck it. They fucked with you." Alex's voice carried over the speakers. A ghost she never expected to hear again, taunting her in a tone she'd never experienced from him. Cold. Cruel. "A quick death is a kindness."

Her stomach lurched, and the little sister in

her whimpered.

"Who is that?" Blake looked at her. "Oh."

She swallowed the bile rising in her throat. She didn't want to hear a replay of Alex's life with Jabberwock.

"This is White Rabbit at his finest." Jabberwock's tone was proud now. Smug. "I hated losing him."

"Then you shouldn't have killed him." Reagan was impressed she managed to keep her voice steady.

"Consider it practice, for what I'm going to do to Blake. Have I ever thanked you for this, Alice? For setting everything in motion? I don't think I have."

She'd promised Blake this asshole wouldn't get in her head. She refused to break that vow, but Jabberwock had a point. Playing a game was her suggestion, back then. It was also a way for her and Blake to get out, so she refused to second-guess the action.

"No comeback? You can do better than that, Alice." Jabberwock sounded disappointed.

She followed Blake, concern growing every time she caught a glimpse of his pinched expression. "Did you really promise my brother you'd keep me safe?" She didn't know why she asked Jabberwock that now. Maybe she hoped she could use it in her favor. It was a stupid thing to wish for, but she didn't have a long list of options.

"I did promise him that. And I am keeping you safe. Watching you grow. Making sure you stay out of the wrong hands," Jabberwock said.

"He took two kilos from your vendor. I think you should get two fingers in return." It was another clip of Alex. It faded into a scream similar to those Blake had let out a few minutes ago.

No. That wasn't her brother suggesting someone lose their digits. It was manufactured. A cruel game.

"We could drop her in Montana," Alex's ghost spoke in a casual tone. "Take her coat and shoes. Ditch her in a snowbank. She tried to set you up."

"*She* was one of Blake's colleagues. You remember her, don't you, Blake? Cute little brunette with the huge… attitude?"

Blake's nostrils flared, but he moved forward.

Reagan was glad she skipped breakfast this morning, as an acrid taste filled her mouth. She checked the next door. *Locked. Go figure.*

"You loved your brother, didn't you?" Jabberwock asked. "Adored him. Spent your adult life looking for ways to avenge him. He'd be so proud of you and what you're becoming."

She bit the inside of her cheek, to keep a retort from slipping out.

"This is where you say, *I'm nothing like that.*" Jabberwock's suggestion added another layer of ice to what was already forming naturally in her veins.

"It sounds like a cheesy movie line, don't you think?"

"Hmm… Good point."
The problem was Reagan worried she might be

exactly like that. If she'd fallen half a step further. If she didn't have Blake to ground her. And she didn't know if she'd moved far enough away from that point to escape it. If she did tumble down that pit, though, she was taking Jabberwock's corpse with her.

Chapter Twenty-Nine

Sawyer sat in the audio booth above the balcony in the high-school auditorium, watching Blake and Alice on the screen in front of him. It was a shame he hadn't had more time to wire the place with cameras and mics, but there was coverage over every square foot, and that would do.

The PA system was shit. However, it did give the whole affair that perfect eerie feeling.

He was disappointed with Blake. He'd expected more of the soldier to kick in, and less of the… whatever Blake had become. It didn't matter. Sawyer would kill the man at the end of the night.

Alice shone, though. Icy. Cool. She'd fumbled with the reminder of her imprisonment but recovered. Fuck—he loved seeing that.

The door clicked behind him. He didn't have to look. Alice and Blake were on-screen, so it would be Lisa.

"You're all set." Her tone was as cool as the air.

He glanced over his shoulder. "Something wrong?"

"Why are we doing this?" she asked.

"It's a game. You know that. Lead the mice through the maze, see how they hunt based on punishment or reward, and pluck Alice out when it's all over."

Lisa frowned. "Like you did with Alex?"

Sawyer was surprised to hear her bring that up, after so long. "Alex had to be punished."

"I loved him, and you knew it."

Sawyer clenched his jaw. "He broke your heart."

"No, he didn't." A sharp edge crept into her voice. "You did, when you killed him."

"You misunderstood. I did that for you. For your sanity." Sawyer set aside his irritation. "I didn't realize you were upset about that still." Alex had threatened to erase Lisa's objectivity. He violated boundaries and tried to steal her away from this. From Wonderland. From the life she loved.

Sawyer hadn't done anything but set him right—show him the error of his ways, before sending him to the next world.

"It's not the kind of thing you just *get over*." Her voice rose in volume. She snapped her mouth shut and glared at him.

"It's been almost six years. He wasn't healthy for you."

"You know what's not healthy?" She was all but shouting. "This fucking obsession you have with *Reagan*."

Sawyer needed to get back to his game. "It's almost over. I promise. Why didn't you tell me you were still upset about him?"

"I should have. You're right." Lisa took a deep breath, and her calm returned. "It's cold, and I'm tired, and we need to deal with Cat, and we're here instead."

"That's fair. We'll go get coffee and soup after this?"

Lisa gave him a warm smile. "All right. Hurry. I mean, as much as is possible."

"Of course." Sawyer returned his attention to the screen, his pawn, and his soon-to-be new queen.

*

Blake hovered on a knife's edge between agony and fury. Watching Reagan's reaction to her brother's voice sliced him from a new direction and left pain the dislocated shoulder couldn't match.

He closed the distance between them, staying on alert while he pressed his good shoulder against her. A trickle of heat—soothing, healing, life giving—flowed between them. That might be a bit melodramatic, but considering the way his arm throbbed with pain, he'd allow himself the indulgence.

"Whatever you hear now doesn't change the person you remember." Blake cringed the moment the words of comfort passed his lips. He'd spoken too loudly.

Reagan gave him a tired smile that vanished a heartbeat later.

"You say that." Jabberwock dragged the words out. "Do you mean it?"

"I do. Besides, the colleague you're

referencing, the cute brunette, didn't freeze to death in a snowbank in Montana. She was tipped off that someone knew about her, and she was pulled from the assignment." Blake motioned down the hallway for them to proceed, and Reagan followed.

The dull look in her eyes worried him.

"My money says he wants you to take that out of context." Blake had no idea whether or not that was true, but for Reagan's sake, he hoped it was.

Jabberwock's laugh clawed down Blake's spine. "You know what the biggest difference between White Rabbit and Hatter was?" Jabberwock asked. "And no, this isn't a riddle. White Rabbit was a sadist, but Hatter was a strategic artist. Everything flowed in front of him like a chessboard. Methodical. Mechanical. Precise."

Blake's shoulder throbbed harder, knocking behind his skull. What else did this lunatic have? There were a lot of things Blake did as Hatter that could be seen as evil and weren't, but just as many that were truly horrific.

Reagan stopped next to Blake again and motioned for him to tilt his head. "We've checked every door," she whispered, "and none of the stairwells up are unlocked."

How had he lost track of that? He wanted to question her observation, but the way his brain swam, he suspected she was more right than he was.

"What now?" She mouthed the words.

"If you block the north, south, and west entrance, you force them out the east." Blake's words mocked him from the speakers. "Let them try to run upstairs, if you want, but funnel them into a wide-open space. Where you have as many hiding spots as they do."

Fucking hell. He knew this scenario, because it was his. A small office building in Shanghai. An executive who threatened to go public with information about Jabberwock. Hatter and Hare were assigned to take care of the problem. It was one of Blake's first tasks after he reached the top, and he'd worked overtime to prove himself.

All the exits downstairs were blocked, though.

So Jabberwock was behind one of the doors they already checked, and Blake would bet it was on this floor. A room with no windows. Possibly the library, if it still had furniture and shelves.

And he assumed Queen was here somewhere. A different room, most likely. Jabberwock might have a screw loose, but he wasn't stupid and wouldn't do this alone. Not like last time.

"Nothing from either of you?" Jabberwock shouted. "Come on."

"*Enough*," Blake barked the word at the same time as Reagan. A trickle of smugness joined his frustration.

"Just one more?" Jabberwock asked.

"No." Blake nodded Reagan toward a door at the other end of the hallway. It was a double door on a short incline. Possibly the entrance to an auditorium.

She took the hint and led the way. When she pushed, unlike last time, the door opened.

They stepped into a small alcove, lights along the floor providing the only illumination. The door swung shut behind them, and he paused while his eyes adjusted to the darkness.

He placed his mouth near her ear. "Next to me at all times. Keep in contact, so we don't lose each other. Stick to the wall."

"Yes," she said.

They crept forward, hugging the carpeting that lined the walls of the room. It was slower going than in the hallway, as he had to check down every aisle of seats. He hated that he couldn't see under them, but unless someone was hiding in the rows, they'd have to scramble out to get to him or Reagan, and that should allow time to react.

They reached the stage after what seemed like an eternity, and moved up slowly.

The pressure against his arm vanished at the same time Reagan gasped. He whirled, to see the curtains next to him flutter and drop back into place. His heart leaped into his throat. "Reagan?" he whispered.

Nothing.

He crept forward and shoved the curtain aside. It was too dark to see anything. The walkway lights didn't reach back here. "*Reagan?*" he shouted into the emptiness.

His voice echoed back. What the fuck was he supposed to do now?

A speaker blared next to his ear, and a screen a few feet away lit up with a projection.

"All right, Mister Bossy." Reagan's voice came from several points at once, and her image flickered onto the screen. She sounded light and playful. A carefree tone Blake had only heard once, when they first met in Las Vegas. He stepped back, to get a better view of the movie.

"*Yes, Sir* will do fine. And think of it as practice for this evening." That was Jabberwock. He stood in what looked like a high-end dressing room, with Reagan, who was undressing.

Blake's nausea grew. He didn't think that was possible.

"Day of the wine tasting." Now-Jabberwock overlapped himself then. "When we all became such good friends."

Blake hadn't forgotten Reagan slept with Jabberwock. He never cared to ask for details, but it wasn't something he resented or blamed her for. That didn't mean he wanted to hear it play out.

"Except I'm not letting you strip me down in a room full of strangers." Her recording, cheerful and on the edge of lust, mocked the pained look she wore these days.

The rage that spilled through Blake burned away the chill and numbed the pain in his shoulder, putting a clarity in his mind that had vanished since they arrived here. In his head, he retraced their steps. He pictured every room, locker, and shift in the wall.

He could go after Reagan, but he didn't know where she was. But Jabberwock was in here. Someplace above the stage. Blake was willing to gamble his life on it. He prayed he wasn't betting Regan's at the same time.

Next question—how was Blake going to get to Jabberwock?

Chapter Thirty

The grip on Reagan's arm was tight, and the hand covering her mouth was calloused It wasn't Jabberwock; she knew that much. A list of options for escape ticked through her head in a blink, and all landed on one conclusion—this was a group of people who didn't hesitate to kill. Pissing them off was a bad idea.

"You saw the photo." Queen's voice was right next to Reagan's head.

Reagan nodded, her pulse hammering in her ears.

"If you promise not to make a sound unless I say it's okay, I can get you out of here alive, and probably Blake too. Deal?"

Reagan questioned a lot of things over the last six months, and made as many mistakes as not when it came to who she trusted, but Queen was *Kitten*, the woman in Alex's journal. Reagan had to take the chance this was a good idea. She nodded.

Queen let go of her, and Reagan whirled. The other woman stood in a casual posture. That didn't mean she had dropped her guard.

"The cameras and microphones are off in here, but it won't be long before Jabberwock figures that out. We don't have much time."

Reagan nodded, keeping her promise not to speak at the front of her mind.

"Blake is right about those clips of Alex. They're out of context. Your brother was the most wonderful man I've ever known. And those clues you've been following? They weren't for you; they were for me."

"But why?" Reagan clapped her hand over her mouth.

Queen gave her a dry smile. "Alex always told me he left proof of everything, *just in case*. He and I knew Jabberwock wasn't stable. Alex said I could go to you, if I needed help figuring things out, but when I sent you the photos after he died, I tracked them. You didn't even open them. Jabberwock was watching you, so I didn't have the option of approaching you back then.

"So I built my own solution," Queen said. "I've been deconstructing things from the inside. Biding my time. Waiting until I could make my move."

A lot of things made sense to Reagan now, but she had so many questions, too. "But you already know everything. Why didn't you destroy Jabberwock yourself?" She wasn't supposed to speak, but Queen didn't look upset at the outburst.

"I don't want to destroy Wonderland; I want to own it. I had to know that what Alex collected wouldn't take it from me if you found it."

"*Lisa.*" Jabberwock's shout filled the air,

ringing in Reagan's head. "It's show time. Are you and your guest ready?"

Queen frowned and drew a pistol from the holster at her hip. "Time's up. I need you to be my prisoner. He'll go for Blake first and make you watch."

"How do you know that?" Regan asked.

"Because it's what he did to me with Alex. He'll kill Blake as slowly as he can, while you watch, and if you don't react the way Jabberwock wants, then you'll be next. If we go now, we might reach Blake before he does."

Reagan could hear the rest later. "I'm your prisoner. Let's go."

Chapter Thirty-One

Sawyer watched on the cameras as Lisa emerged from the room she held Alice in. Desire, white and hot, ripped through his veins. Soon, Alice would be his. She'd see that Blake wasn't worth her effort.

Alice would yield to Sawyer, the way she had in the dressing room. At the masquerade. Every time she encountered him.

He double-checked, to ensure his holster was secure and that he carried a blade in his inside jacket pocket.

If Alice the insignificant mites that was Blake, they could die together.

But she was Sawyers. The way Lisa was. He'd have his White Queen and his Queen of Hearts, and together, they'd watch anyone burn who dared stand in their way.

Chapter Thirty-Two

Blake crept up the ramp to the balcony, keeping his back to the wall and watching ahead and behind him at the same time, as much as one man was able.

A movement on the lower end of the ramp caught his attention, and he spun as Queen and Reagan moved into view. He raised his pistol at the same time Queen did, but something behind him creaked. Leather, followed by a metal *snap*.

Blake spun back toward the noise, to see Jabberwock aim at him. *Fuck.*

Queen pressed her gun into Reagan's temple. "I'm guessing the two of you are fucking. Tell me, Blake. The entire time you were together, you never taught your sweet Alice to watch her six?"

Blake clenched his jaw and tightened his grip on his weapon. Could he hit Queen before she pulled the trigger? Hell, he didn't even know if he could get his arm up that fast.

Jabberwock paced. The scene was too familiar to six months ago. Blake feeling like someone had forgotten to let him in on the joke, and not seeing a lot of options for escape.

"Injured arm, aiming with your left, could you still hit me before I hit you?" Jabberwock studied Blake. His gun remained in its familiar shoulder holster. Jabberwock reached for it, and Blake twitched his finger.

"Nuh-uh." Jabberwock held his hands in the air. "Not yet."

Reagan whimpered.

"Don't," Queen barked. "There's no love lost between you and me, and unlike the two of them, I won't hesitate to drop you."

Fuck, fuckity fuck fuck. Blake would never forgive himself if he got Reagan killed.

Jabberwock laughed. "*Fuck.* I love this woman. Not the same way I love you, Alice, but there's a great deal of professional respect there. This afternoon, I set the rules, and they're simple. Blake has one bullet. If he shoots me, Alice dies. Queen isn't big on torture, so she's going to pull the trigger immediately.

"If Blake shoots her first, Reagan lives. I kill Blake, and her reaction dictates how much longer she continues to live. I'm not stupid. I already know the hero is going to sacrifice himself to save the girl. Since he's fucked either way… What'll it be, Blake? Kill me and watch Reagan die, or take the coward's way out and get yourself killed before she shows the rest of us she was only using you?"

If there was a chance of Reagan escaping, Blake was going to take it. That meant figuring out how he could shoot Queen. Even as recently as a week ago, Blake would have questioned where Reagan's loyalty lay after a speak like that from

Jabberwock. He didn't doubt now. She wouldn't side with the psychopath, but she would do what it took to save herself.

That was Blake's only option. He just didn't know how to distract Queen long enough to shoot her.

She drew back the hammer on her pistol, and his concern grew.

The entire time Blake had known Queen, regardless of what she called herself, he'd never seen her cock the hammer on her gun before she fired. Was this her way of proving Jabberwock's point?

In a blink, she raised her gun in his direction. He twitched to counter and return fire, but he was slow with his left arm. The gunshot exploded, ringing in his ears.

If he could still hear, and think, she didn't shoot him. Warning shot? Where was the mocking from Jabberwock?

Queen let go of Reagan, and Blake risked a glance over his shoulder. Jabberwock's body lay on the round, dark red oozing from the hole in his head.

Blake dropped the Glock with one bullet, pulled Jabberwock's from its holster, and shot the body twice in the chest and once more in the head.

"Feel better?" Queen asked.

Blake aimed at her. She raised her hands, letting her trigger-guard hang from her forefinger.

"What the fuck was that?" he asked.

"Exactly what it looks like." Queen handed her sidearm to Reagan and took another step back.

Reagan set the weapon on the ground.

Blake was pretty sure the pain in his shoulder

was making him hallucinate.

"It's over. You can walk away. Actually leave. No games. No *I'll look for you in six months*," Queen said.

Blake blinked and shook his head, to clear out the bizarre fantasy. He pinched himself then looked at her. "You're still here. Not a dream after all."

Queen rolled her eyes. "You've never been funny."

"What am I missing?" Blake was so tired of mind games.

"She's Cheshire Cat," Reagan said.

"Actually, I'm Lisa. Please—*God*—don't call me by another of those stupid names." She reached behind her.

Blake evened off the gun again. "Careful."

Lisa presented an envelope. "It's not loaded." She rifled through it and plucked out a photograph. "This is mine. The rest is yours." She handed it to Reagan.

"Thank you." Reagan took the offering. "For this. For that." She nodded at Jabberwock. "I don't suppose... Do you have the password I need for the decryption key?"

"You mean the one Alex left for me? I'll let you keep the data, but hear me out first."

"I don't understand why we're hearing anything. Why are we standing here, talking like old friends?" Blake asked.

"I trust her." Reagan made it sound obvious.

"Why?"

"I'm a little naive sometimes." Reagan shrugged, a smile playing on her face. "But she's seen a lot. Alex trusted her. Alex loved her."

"Alex died for me. And I'm so sorry that, in doing so, he set you on this path." Lisa looked at Reagan. The stony mask was gone, replaced with the same exhaustion that dragged through Blake.

He was still missing something. "I'm sorry. Bad guy's dead, right? So, no more looking glass? No more fucking with our heads."

Lisa rubbed her arms and pulled her coat more tightly around her. "I have no idea how you two aren't shivering your asses off. I've been playing the long game, waiting for this day. I cleared you five years ago, when Sawyer—him"—she nodded at Jabberwock—"needed someone new to replace White Rabbit. I made sure your NSA records vanished, because you had potential."

"Why?"

"Because he killed Alex. Tortured. Destroyed. Obliterated. That was another one of his games. You had the ability to take him down, if I nudged you right. You were so close, and then you had to go and fuck his latest obsession, and it all crumbled. He closed ranks. Until you and Reagan brought things back on track. Thank you, by the way, for turning disaster into another distraction."

"You're welcome?" That was the correct response, wasn't it? He should be asking more questions or something, but he was using the last of his energy to fend off the pain and cold.

"The doors are locked from the outside," Reagan said. "Unless you have a magic switch?"

"Sort of." Lisa pulled her phone from her pocket, jabbed the screen a few times, then put it away again. "Ten—Trinity is her real name—is an old friend. She's out there. Doors are open now. Take Blake someplace warmer before he collapses? Your car is outside. I drove it here." She handed Reagan a familiar key ring. "The encryption key is *kitten*. Like it sounds. All lower case. It's up to you what you do with the data, but Jabberwock doesn't exist anymore, and in about twelve hours, Cheshire Cat won't either. And the three of us… We'll never see each other again."

Blake should do more. Say more. "That's it?"

"You're still a fugitive. I can't fix that if you stand here, chatting my ear off."

"You're sure?" He couldn't help his sarcasm. "You don't have another magic switch in your phone?"

Reagan walked to his side and took his hand. "Let's go."

Her comfort with the situation didn't stop him from glancing over his shoulder every other second, as they made their way downstairs and outside, but he noticed she did the same. They reached the car without further incident. Their coats were piled in the back seat. She handed him his and pulled hers on.

"A little help?" It was silly to feel embarrassed to ask, after everything else that had transpired, but he was.

Reagan assisted him in shrugging on the coat, taking extra care with his lame arm. The fabric was as icy as the air, but it started to warm the moment it was on.

He leaned back against the car and wrapped

his good arm around her waist. "That just happened? It's over?" he asked.

"As far as I can tell."

"Christ, that man was fucked up." He didn't have anything more profound to say about the situation.

She leaned in, to brush her lips over his. "And gone. And we need to leave too."

He nodded and slid into the passenger seat, while she took point as driver.

"Where to?" Reagan pulled onto the road. "I believe I was promised a plane to Fiji."

He remembered saying that. Out of everything that transpired since this morning, it was the one thing that sounded normal. "Get me a burner phone at the nearest convenience station, and Fiji it is." He'd place a call to Ephraim, make good on his promise a few weeks late, and they'd go wait for their ride at the Logan airport. No reason to go back for their things. Nothing in the room was important.

Reagan set her arm on the rest between them, and he grasped her hand. Her fingers warmed against his, and she spared him a tiny smile.

He had no idea if they could put this behind them, but he was done pursuing it, and if she felt the same, maybe they had a chance to move on. He studied her profile in the fading light—fierce but still fragile, and the most stunning sight in his memory. He definitely hoped they could move on.

Epilogue

Reagan closed her eyes as a gust of ocean air swirled around her, tearing her hair from her face and leaving hints of salt on her skin. She tried to absorb it a piece at a time, but it all blurred together. She came out here most mornings, to do a half-assed form of meditation. Mostly, it was standing on the beach and losing herself in the crash of the surf and the rustle of the palm-tree leaves.

Blake wrapped his arms around her from behind and kissed along her shoulder. "See anything interesting?"

"Absolutely nothing." She looked at the crystal-blue water, licking up the sand but not quite reaching her toes.

"Hmm…" He slid a finger under the string holding up her bikini top. "Sounds stunning."

"It is. More amazing than any poet would ever lead you to believe *nothing* could be." It had been almost a year since the incident at the high school. The dreams that woke her up in a cold sweat, where she swore the walls were closing in and the only thing she heard was Jabberwock's voice, had faded. They only came every few weeks now.

She traced her fingers over the familiar inlay of the silver locket that rested at the base of her throat. The necklace didn't hold photos of her or Blake—they avoided having their pictures taken. Nestled inside was the silicon-encased micro SD card with the layout of Sawyer Brolin's financial holdings. Several of which had *mysteriously* vanished or were sold to another holding company in the last eleven months.

Reagan and Blake had evidence that Lisa was transferring all of Sawyer's dealings to be under a new pseudonym, but Reagan hadn't pushed to find out more than that. So far, there was no reason to.

"Breakfast is ready when you are," Blake said.

It was one of the thousands of things Reagan discovered about him once they had time to talk— the man was a wicked cook. Which was good. She'd spent more time learning to hack than to boil water, so her best contribution to food was ordering pizza online. "I could be persuaded to eat."

He turned her to face him. "*Persuaded*?" He tangled his fingers in her hair and crushed his mouth to hers. The intensity of the kiss stole her breath and mingled with the peace in her head rather than disrupting it.

When he broke away, she let a shy grin slip out. In a previous life, she would have felt obligated to flirt after a gesture like that. Come back with something like, *Am I breakfast?* With Blake, that need to pretend was gone.

This was right. Some days life was still

terrifying, but on those days, everything startled her. Most of the time, things with Blake were good. More than she ever dared hope for.

He tangled his fingers in hers and tugged her toward their cottage. As they approached, she caught a reflection of herself in the glass. Her hair was growing out red again. It was at about her ears now, leaving an odd stripe of blonde at the bottom. Dye it to match never felt like a priority.

They stepped inside, and a sparkle caught her attention. She turned toward the living room, and saw the small rubber plant they kept in the corner was strung with lights. A few boxes sat next to the pot, wrapped in bright paper. "What did you do?" she asked.

"Merry Christmas."

"It's only Halloween," she pointed out.

"I know, but we missed Thanksgiving and Christmas last year, because mental and physical agony, and now that we're getting better at this living life thing…" He brushed past her, grabbed one of the smaller boxes, and handed it to her. "Short version is, I couldn't wait. I'm also not the kind of poet who can make *nothing* sound any more tempting than you did outside, so… open it?"

Her voice jammed in her throat, as she tore off the shiny red wrapper to expose a black velvet box. She opened it and gasped at the sight of a thin silver bracelet with *Reagan* etched on it. She still introduced herself as Alice, but he always called her by her real name, when they were alone. "It's beautiful."

He dragged a thumb across her cheek,

smudging wetness over her skin. "I didn't think I'd get tears out of you."

"Well you did." She shook her head and pulled away, to draw the back of her hand over her face. She didn't know if either of them would ever stop looking over their shoulder. They'd be keeping a loose eye on Lisa Haynes or whoever replaced her for the rest of their lives. But if Reagan had Blake, the rest would fall into place somehow.

THE END

www.ingramcontent.com/pod-product-compliance
Lightning Source LLC
Chambersburg PA
CBHW050400190726
48284CB00007BB/2374